Alel is a demon, and he is good at lying. The image he wears is a lie—no one can see his wings or barbed tail, nor can they see the horns peeking from a shag of hair salted with strands of white and pale gray. Half-starved, Alel is short and gangly and has lavender freckles dusted across his nose and cheeks. Lust created him along with all other incubi and succubae for one reason—to encourage humans to sin while feeding off of their sexual energy. Anything more than carnal acts is forbidden, but Alel yearns to be kissed, to bury his face in the crook of a lover's neck and hold them until dawn.

When he meets a human named Jackson, who's more interested in snuggling on the couch while watching movies and making out instead of one-night stands, Alel realizes dating Jackson would leave him famished, but he can't resist the temptation.

As their relationship builds, Alel and Jackson explore the boundaries of both sexual and romantic intimacy. The more they're together, the more they fall in love, but Alel knows if another demon ever catches him, he'll be dragged back to hell for breaking taboo.

SAVED BY GRACE

Sita Bethel

A NineStar Press Publication

Published by NineStar Press
P.O. Box 91792,
Albuquerque, New Mexico, 87199 USA.
www.ninestarpress.com

Saved by Grace

Printed in the USA
First Edition
December, 2018

Print ISBN: 978-1-949909-56-2

Also available in eBook, ISBN: 978-1-949909-49-4

Warning: This book contains sexually explicit content, which may only be suitable for mature readers, graphic violence, and attempted rape.

This one's for the guardian angel who helps me
outline all my stories.

Chapter One

ALEL WAS A demon, and he was good at lying. The image he wore was a lie, a specific one called a glamour that allowed him to appear to others however he wanted. His favorite human persona was teak-skinned with olive eyes and braids like so many tiny garden snakes. To any passerby, he was tall and sculpted, confident and relaxed, dangerous and mysterious, and it was all a pretty lie.

No one could see the wings or the barbed tail, nor could anyone see the horns peeking from a shag of hair salted with strands of white and pale gray. He was short, and gangly, and had lavender freckles dusted across his nose and cheeks. No one would want him as his true self, but Alel was a demon, and he was good at lying.

He stood veiled in cigarette smoke. He didn't drink; it was too hard to hold the glamour if he was drunk. Instead, Alel leaned against a wall with his arms crossed. He scanned the party crowd, searching for someone to take home for the night. Incubi were children of Lust; they fed off desire and satisfaction the way human infants survived off their mother's milk—by suckling the nourishment straight from the flesh.

He saw Naberius walking out of the throng of people with a human slung around his arm. They stumbled, both drunk and laughing. Unlike Alel, Naberius loved to drink and eat. His glamour persona was a rugged, tanned gym fanatic, but in reality, he had quite the pooch in his belly from taking lovers three or four at a time, and by the gleam in his stark blue eyes, Alel could tell he was in no mood for a single lover that night.

"Lonely?" Naberius winked, licking his lips afterward.

"Never." Alel snorted, although in truth, he was lonelier than he could bear, but no amount of one-night stands could fix the hollow space inside him.

"Well, my friend here is." Naberius pinched the human's ass. "Want to go back to my place, Al?"

Alel sized up the human. He wore thick-framed, bright-red glasses and looked candid. Alel was fond of virgins; they were bashful and responded nicely when he brushed his fingers against their skin. Alel cupped the man's face and caressed his thumb across the human's cheek.

"Do you want me to come?" Alel asked, his voice sultry and inviting because he was good at lying.

The human turned away. He blushed and nodded his head. Naberius gestured toward the door and Alel followed them. Naberius's Ferrari Lusso sat double-parked in the handicapped zone. They climbed into the car and took off at whatever speed Naberius fancied.

Alel struggled not to roll his eyes. It was all so cliché he couldn't stand it. Yet another demon with an expensive, red car—why always candy-apple red? It was like they were afraid driving a white car would somehow turn them into an angel. Yet another demon driving without any regard to the speed limit. Every demon Alel knew was the same, and he could never figure out why they thought speeding made them more *evil*. Speeding was illegal, but it wasn't a sin. However, no matter how many times Alel explained this, his consorts always argued with him, saying it proved they were superior to humans because they didn't have to follow human laws. They didn't have to break them, either, if they were above them, but that was an unpopular opinion, and Alel seemed to be the only one afflicted with it.

They both escorted their human meal into Naberius's apartment and straight to his bed. Without ceremony, they tugged off every scrap of clothing between the three of them and lay the human on black satin sheets—which was also cliché—why was it always red sports cars and black satin sheets? Alel wanted to scream.

"Do your thing." Naberius grinned.

Alel gazed at the human. The man's eyes were a warm hazel color. Alel caressed his cheek again. The incubus was awful at hunting and was half-starved because of it, but Alel had a strange talent for calming virgins, so Naberius often invited Alel to share meals to take advantage of his skill. It wasn't hard to seduce a shy human. Alel relished the time it took, talking to them, touching them little by little, watching and listening for nonverbal queuing and giving them what they were too nervous to vocalize. The fun of a meal came from the anticipation of the first taste, and Alel enjoyed the mouthwatering moment before feeding more so than he ever enjoyed the main course.

Alel leaned down, almost brushing his lips against the drunk, hazel-eyed human. A wicked, imaginary tug pulled his lips close to his prey's, but he never indulged the urge to kiss because kissing was an act of love and therefore forbidden to him. Teasing, on the other hand, was permitted, and teasing always made humans arch up and whimper, *begging* for what Alel held out of their grasp.

And they had to beg. The human had to *want it*. Desire was important. An incubus offered what a human already craved and guided them, gently and sweetly, away from God and toward anything else. Lust, Greed, Sloth, Envy, Avarice, Wrath, and Pride: those sins were the parents of every demon and who the demons answered to if they failed to create discord in the world.

"Are you nervous?" Alel ran the pad of his thumb across the human's bottom lip instead of kissing him.

"A little," the human gasped, already hitching up and trying to grind their bodies together.

"Don't worry." Alel palmed the human's erection. "We're going to make you feel amazing."

He wasn't lying. The more eager the prey, the better the meal. Alel teased his lips above the human's body, enjoying the way the human's eyes lidded and how his breathing sped up the more Alel taunted him. He could have gone for hours, touching and toying with the human until he was so ready only a few strokes of Alel's hand would be enough to undo him, but Naberius didn't have the patience for it. He knelt on the bed behind Alel and rammed his cock into Alel's ass without foreplay or warning.

"Naberius!" Alel gasped, clenching on reflex.

"Couldn't help myself. You were too cute kneeling on all fours." Naberius set up a rhythm.

Alel groaned, adjusting right away to Naberius's fast speed and thick girth. He groaned and yanked at the sheets below. Remembering their prey, he collected himself and focused back on the human. Alel reached for the lube Naberius kept on hand for mortal lovers. He coated his fingers and reached between the man's legs. He only rubbed around the human's entrance, letting him adjust to the sensation. As he toyed with the human's asshole, Alel sucked hard enough on his prey's skin to leave dark red-violet reminders of the night across the man's chest. The stranger held Alel's shoulders and arched. Alel kept sucking— sucking, not kissing—until his meal was clawing at Alel's shoulders and gasping.

The human's sharp intake of breath excited Alel, and the more Naberius pounded into Alel from behind, the more Alel wanted it. Each thrust hit his prostate and made him forget everything except how good he felt. He doused his fingers with another round of lube and pressed one into the human's body. He didn't squirm or whimper at one finger, so Alel added a second, making his "supper" moan as Alel worked his fingers in and out. The human slammed his eyes shut and lolled his head from side to side.

"Grab my cock," Alel instructed, pulling his hand away.

The human shifted so he could wrap his hand around Alel's shaft.

"Good. Firm. Just like that. Now make me come."

"Don't worry, Al. You know I can last all night." Naberius laughed, tugging Alel's hair back and slamming into his ass harder.

Alel called out, relaxing and giving himself over to Naberius's whims, but he managed to angle his head toward his human despite Naberius's claws in his hair.

"But I want *you* to do it," he whispered to the human. "*You.* Touch me. Make me come."

Something changed in the human's expression, a shift from passive to active. He *wanted them.* Alel saw it glinting in the human's eyes, bright as hellfire. The human started stroking Alel's cock, dragging little moans from Alel's mouth with each jerk of his hand.

Alel pulled away from both of them, rolling over and situating the human on top. He rubbed lube on the human's cock until it shined and then spread his legs wide. Naberius pouted as he watched, temperamental about the switch but silent because he knew the more engaged the human, the more energy they could siphon from him.

The human held his cock as he tried to push into Alel's body. He struggled, too gentle at first, but Alel's asshole yielded, sucking in the human's hard flesh and clinging around his shaft.

"O-oh God," the human moaned.

"Good, right?" Naberius purred in the human's ear, spurred on by the mild blasphemy.

Alel caught Naberius staring at him, but the moment his gaze locked onto Naberius's, Naberius jerked away. Meanwhile, the human pulled out and slipped back in. His thrusts were shaky and inexperienced, but the energy he put out was delicious, and Alel licked his lips, savoring the flavor of lust filling his mouth. He tasted strawberry cake and thick buttercream frosting, and Alel sighed as he fed off the human's need to fuck.

"God, oh God. Shit."

He tried stroking Alel, but as the human drew close to orgasm, he forgot about Alel's cock and sped up, lost in his own pleasure.

It was delicious. It'd been so long since Alel last ate that any scrap of food was delicious.

"Fuck...fuck..." the human sped up, hips moving in quick jerks. "Jesus Christ!" He threw his head back and screamed as he came.

Naberius grabbed the human and pulled him close, shoving in. The human moaned, sweat dripping down his temples. Alel smiled at the way the human's hair matted to his forehead and the way he wrinkled his face. He never tired of watching his lover's' faces as they forgot their lives and forfeited to the moment. Naberius didn't last long, going quick and hard and then hissing and dropping to his mattress.

His chest expanded and collapsed, and his eyes stayed closed. Alel knew he wouldn't receive satisfaction from Naberius. The other demon was fed and sexually satisfied; he didn't care about what Alel and the human did for the rest of the night. The human gave Alel a sheepish glance, noticing his erection standing—tall and black from the human's point of view, although in truth it was a pillar of marble and not jet.

"Touch me," Alel whispered again.

The human crawled toward him, gripping Alel's cock and stroking it once more. He was handsome, this sweat-baptized human stroking Alel's cock. Alel risked reaching up and combing his fingers through the human's hair, smiling at the soft expression his touch brought to the human's face.

"What's your name?" Alel asked.

"Don't name the food, Al," Naberius grumbled, turning on his side away from them.

"Is he still drunk?" the human asked.

"I think so." Alel laughed.

"Daniel," the human said.

"I really want to come, Daniel." Alel hummed, easing into the mattress and hitching into Daniel's hand.

"O-okay," Daniel said with a shaky breath, nervous as he stroked Alel as quickly as his wrist could move.

He'd drunk in more energy than he had in months, but he kept feeding and couldn't stop. Alel knew it might be a while until he ate again—probably the next time Naberius needed a wingman—so he wanted to take all he could get. Alel traced his fingers across Daniel's shoulders. Daniel smiled at the light touches. Alel held his breath, his orgasm welling up from inside. After a final moan, come spilled over the tip of Alel's cock onto Daniel's wrist.

Alel gave the human an appreciative hum. He muttered the human's name, holding his hand and licking the come off the human's wrist. When he finished, Daniel snuggled up beside him. Alel shot a nervous glance at Naberius, but the other incubus was snoring on his side and oblivious to them. He figured he could indulge the human. What was the harm? It made the human happy, made him prone to the idea of future meals, right? As long as Naberius didn't see, as long as no other demons saw the moment of affection, it should be all right.

Alel dozed, waking up with a start as a car backfired from the street outside Naberius's bedroom window. He slipped out from under Daniel's hold, knowing it was dangerous to linger in his embrace, and used Naberius's shower. Towel wrapped around his waist, Alel searched for his clothes among the piles scattered around the bedroom floor.

"You always sneak away afterward." Naberius kept his eyes closed as he spoke.

"There's no reason to stay." Alel slipped into his pants.

"Breakfast."

"I'm good."

"You're scrawny as fuck." Naberius opened his eyes. "Come back to bed and feed again in the morning—hell, we can wake him up for round two now if you want."

"Let him sleep." Alel wrestled into his shirt and fastened his belt. He searched the room for his shoes, forcing himself not to look at Naberius.

"Alel—"

"What? I'll grab something to snack on later. I'm fine." Alel gave Daniel one last glance.

"Stop it," Naberius growled.

"Jealous?" Alel sat beside Naberius and wiggled his feet into his socks. Naberius's fingers curled around Alel's wrist. Their gazes met again, an echo from earlier in bed only this time Naberius didn't turn away, Alel did. "Thanks for sharing dinner with me."

Alel left them both. He didn't want to be there in the morning, not even for the meal. He couldn't say goodbye. His lovers always had the same sad expression when he left, and he hated it. He *should relish in it*. Alel existed in the world only to give humans pain, but it left a curdled taste in his mouth. He preferred strawberry cake and fucking to sour milk and goodbyes. Learning their names made it worse. He knew better, *don't name the food*, but he always wanted to say it: their names.

Alel reached the bus stop, and he sat on the bench, wanting an excuse to stare at the city as it slept. The sky hovered dark but graying, in preparation for dawn. A garbage truck beeped along the street, clanging a heavy, metal dumpster as it tipped the bin upside down to unload it.

"I always catch you waiting for the sunrise." The angel sat next to Alel as if they were buddies instead of ancient foes in an eternal battle.

"Go away, Sariel."

"It's funny."

"What's funny?"

"I've never met a demon who used my name. The others use terms of blasphemy."

"I save the blasphemy for the bedroom."

"Yes, I heard. You also used their names, the human's name and Naberius's."

"It's erotic."

"Hmmm...I guess. I wouldn't know."

Alel snuck a quick peek at Sariel. He hated looking at angels because they were beautiful. He imagined tying up the one beside him with white, silk rope and a satin blindfold. Once he had the angel helpless, he'd find out how much torment an angel could stand; rose petals against the skin, feathers along the stomach, soft fur against the thighs, an ice cube against the nipples. Alel could spend an entire night making his holy captive writhe against the bonds.

Alel jumped into the angel's lap and leaned close. He cupped the angel's chin with thumb and forefinger, tilting the angel's head up and staring into their eyes.

"Want to know? I could show you."

"You think so? You do realize angels are androgynous, don't you? There's nothing for you to fuck."

"Everyone knows that, but if you called out to God in a moment of lust, then I still win, and I don't need to make you come to ruin you." Alel grinned. "Making an angel fall would taste better than a hundred human orgasms. Custard, I think, creme brulée."

Sariel mirrored Alel's smile in his own expression. He reached up and held Alel's face. The angel brushed their noses together, and Alel's stomach looped.

"Does this mean you are coming home with me?"

"Kiss me, Alel," Sariel whispered.

"W-what?" His heart rioted in his chest, and his breath evaporated in his throat. He became dizzy and shaky.

Sariel hovered his lips over Alel's. "I said kiss me. I want you to kiss me."

Alel's lips parted in anticipation. Blood pooled into his cock, and it throbbed from want. Alel pulled back, eyes squeezed shut as he turned away.

"Are you trying to get my mouth stuffed with scorpions and sewn shut? You know I can't kiss you."

"And I can't say the Lord's name in vain in a moment of passion. If you want to ruin me, why shouldn't I ruin you back?"

"Because your side is more forgiving."

Sariel's hand returned to his cheek, and he started, glancing back at the angel and wishing he hadn't because the sky was glowing orange all around them, which made the holy creature even more beautiful.

"Alel, do you realize any other demon would have said no because kissing was filthy, not because they'd get punished for it?"

"It is filthy," he whispered, brushing his lips with the tips of his fingers and trembling at the sensitive touch. "All the spit, and smashing faces together. It's absurd. Who'd willingly subject themselves to that?"

"I want to give you something," Sariel said.

"No, I don't trust you."

"Take it." The angel held out a scrap of paper.

"What is it?"

"The address and date of a party."

"Are you asking me on a date?"

"It's a human party." The angel laughed. "I think you might be able to find something better than a quick meal there."

"Am I so skinny even angels are trying to feed me now?"

"Yes," Sariel said.

"I don't need charity from *you*."

"Alel, you're so unhappy it makes me sad, and an angel should never feel sorrow for a demon."

"I don't believe this." Alel stood up, walking home with his head bent low.

The angel ran after him. "There's no tricks. I promise! It's a party a human I watch over got invited to. I think you two would get along well. He's not happy either, and I can't interfere directly, but if things happened on their own? There's no harm in it, right?"

"Are you out of your mind?" Alel stopped, pivoting and turning to glare at Sariel. "You're looking after a human who's sad and your master plan is to let a demon feed off his soul? You're sicker than my kind."

"I believe everything will turn out in the end." The angel smiled.

Alel snatched the paper from the angel's hand. "I hope I do find this human. I'm going to fuck his brains out until he dies of dehydration and laugh in your face because it'll be your fault for giving me this address."

The angel laughed and laughed until they had to support themself by propping their hands against their knees.

"What's so funny?"

"Nothing!" the angel laughed.

"Are angels supposed to lie?"

"It's not funny, it's simply...ironic, but good luck. You'll need it."

"What's that supposed to mean?"

"Nothing."

"You're lying again." Alel frowned.

"I guess I shouldn't hang out with demons, then." Sariel leaned forward, stealing a kiss from Alel's cheek. "You're a bad influence on me. I'll see you around."

Alel rubbed his cheek, but the strange, tingling lingered on his skin. He growled in frustration. His hard-on still pressed against his pants, and he couldn't shake the enticing thoughts from earlier. He imagined the squeal of delight the angel would make as Alel sucked on their toes, or nibbled their ear, or sucked on their nipples—if angels had nipples. Alel wasn't sure, but he wanted to suck on them, anyway.

He reached his apartment complex. Inside he saw a woman leaning against the wall smoking a cigarette. She glanced at him and smiled. Alel remembered he was still wearing his glamour, so she couldn't see the dark circles beneath his eyes or his sallow cheeks. He licked his lips, tasting her attraction on the tip of his tongue. The taste was pure, white sugar.

He knew what he should do, walk up to her, say hi, lead her to the laundry room and bend her over a washing machine. He was a fucking incubus. He was created for no other purpose than fucking and draining humans of their energy. He was malnourished and needed to eat more because even angels were starting to pity him.

But he was tired.

He had just eaten.

She wasn't half as pretty as the angel had been, so why bother?

He ran to his apartment and flung himself onto his bed, dropping the ridiculous glamour and feeling more himself after it was gone. Alel groaned, his weight pressing his arousal against the mattress. He was good at lying, even to himself. He wasn't too tired. He'd eaten, but he was still hungry. Sariel *was* prettier, but that wasn't exactly why he wasn't interested in the woman downstairs. Alel went back to thoughts of dragging rose petals across Sariel's wrists and stomach. He hitched forward, sighing at the friction and the way it made him shudder. Naberius always finished too quickly, and Alel was always hungry afterward. He thought of the woman again but only wrinkled his face.

"Go fuck her," Alel growled into his pillow, even as he hitched against the mattress again.

It'd be nice, the rush of wet and hot surrounding his cock, the slapping sound of flesh on flesh as he smacked against her ass with each thrust. He wanted it. He wanted it, so why did he keep hitching against the mattress and thinking about it instead of going back downstairs?

He blamed Sariel. Who'd want to fuck a human after sitting in an angel's lap? He kept thinking about the curves of Sariel's face, the plumpness of the angel's lips, the way the angel tilted their head up and asked to be kissed.

Alel groaned, rolling over, undoing his fly, and grabbing hold of his burning-hot cock. He squeezed, thumbing around the edge of his cockhead. Alel spread out his wings, tossing his head from side to side.

He told himself to stop. He couldn't feed himself. He needed to go and find a partner or even two. He could be like Naberius and get chubby, with a lover wrapped around each arm, but his hand felt so good on his cock, and he was imagining how soft Sariel's lips would be against his.

He winced, not wanting to accept the daydream, not able to resist it. He wanted to kiss. He wanted to brush his lips against another's while his fingers sifted through their hair. He wanted slow, lasting, sweet sex instead of the constant rush of successive, quick romps, and he hated himself for wanting things he couldn't have.

Chapter Two

JACKSON SEARCHED THE room for someone interesting to talk to. People stared at him, smiled, one woman winked. They were all drunk from the party and wanting Jackson for something he wouldn't give them. He wanted conversation. Real fucking make-you-think conversation and not small talk.

He saw a sweet little piece of eye candy brooding by himself on a faded green loveseat in the den. The fact that he was alone intrigued Jackson, and he meandered closer. As he approached, the faint but telltale tingle of magic vibrated against his skin. The man on the loveseat was hiding behind a glamour.

Jackson grinned. He'd dated vampires in the past and wouldn't mind offering a little blood for a few nights of good company. He marched toward the couch, plopping close to the vampire and leaning closer.

"Are you as bored as I am?"

The man started, jerking his head in Jackson's direction. He appeared to be puzzled that someone had spoken to him. Jackson wondered if Mr. Tall Dark And Handsome was new to the undead scene because he didn't have the confidence of any of the vampires Jackson had ever met.

"Yeah, a friend convinced me to give this party a try, but I'm not in the mood for socializing tonight."

"I know what you mean." Jackson nodded. "I'd rather be at home on my own couch."

"You ever think about how we pay to live in a space and pay even more money to get away from it? Why do people bother?"

"Good point. Guess it's human nature to think the grass is greener on the other side." Jackson grinned. "What's your name?"

"People call me Al."

"Hey, Al. I'm Jackson." He reached out his hand.

Al stared at their clasped hands as if it were his first handshake.

"So what would you rather be doing right now?" Jackson asked.

"Sleeping." Al snorted.

Jackson laughed. He'd expected a different answer, something more exciting. He took a swallow from his beer, peering into the crowd. Everyone looked the same to Jackson: different shirts, different accessories, but each male had the same tan and the same haircut and the same drunk smile. Someone might as well have dumped a pile of Ken dolls on the floor. The women were a little varied, but only as much as Barbie and Courtney. It made his brain hurt when he thought about it.

"I honestly don't have anything better to do than be here. I guess that's the problem." Jackson sank back into the couch a little more.

"It always amazes me how much time people waste when the human lifespan is already too short."

"So what the hell have you accomplished in your life?" Jackson snorted.

"Nothing."

"Okay, then."

"I can play the violin," Al said in a timid voice, as if he didn't want Jackson to hear the words.

"No shit?"

He nodded.

"That's cool. Did your mom make you take lessons or something?"

"No." Al gave him a quick, bitter laugh. "My mother's a whore. If I'm out of sight, I'm out of mind. I learned because I wanted to."

"Yeah, mine was a drunk. She had a different guy every week. Didn't know my father. You?"

"Not really."

"Siblings?"

"More than I can count. They're all assholes, though."

"I'm an only child." Jackson sucked from the mouth of his beer bottle.

From the narrow view from the doorway, they could see a drunk couple pressed against the wall, biting each other's necks and groping wherever their hands could reach.

"Damn, they're just gonna go right at it in front of everyone." Jackson shook his head.

"Does it bother you?" Al raised an eyebrow.

"It's not my thing, but it doesn't bother me." Jackson shrugged. He glanced at his companion, grinning. "You're getting off on this, aren't you?"

"A little," his reply was cool, nonchalant. "It's hard not to watch without thinking about how it feels."

"Can't be that good. They're drunk."

"You know the saying. Sex is like pizza."

"When it's good, it's really good, but when it's bad—it's still pretty good," Jackson quoted.

"Yeah."

"You've obviously never tried my homemade pizza. It invalidates the entire argument."

Al grinned. "Are you inviting me over to your place for pizza?"

"Actually, pizza does sound good." Jackson stopped, thinking a moment. "We *are* talking about pizza, right?"

"It is the topic of conversation."

"Because I wasn't trying to invite you over for amazing sex, or anything. I actually want pizza now."

"Amazing, you say?"

"Amazing pizza."

"Okay, amazing pizza, hold the double entendre." Al sat in silence for a moment, working his mouth as if he were trying to chew on the proposal. Then he shrugged.

"Fuck it, why not? Save me from this pathetic party."

"Okay, let's go."

A rush of excitement flooded through Jackson as they walked outside. The thought of hanging out and cooking pizza and eating while talking sounded great.

"We could watch a movie while we eat. What's your favorite movie genre? Don't worry, I'll be sure to skip the garlic when I make the pizza."

"Um, sure? I...actually, I can't remember the last time I saw a movie? Vincent Price movies are good."

"Those are classics. Let's watch *Theatre of Blood.*"

They walked to the nearest store for supplies and took an Uber back to Jackson's apartment. Jackson made sure to cross the threshold first, bowing and gesturing into his home.

"Please, come inside," he said, inviting the vampire into the apartment.

"Thanks." Al stepped through the doorway, admiring the pictures on the walls.

"I took those myself."

"Really?"

"Yeah. Professionally, I take pictures of models, but I prefer regular people."

Jackson started unpacking groceries on the island counter separating the kitchen and living room.

"The camera catches the real honesty in people in a way they don't see on their own. It's a shame we ruin the truth with airbrushing and Photoshop."

"Hmmm, I agree. I love observing people. They're more beautiful than they know." Al sat on a stool, elbows on the counter and cradling his chin. He snorted, turning away. "Never mind, that was stupid. I'm not sure why I said it."

"That's exactly what I meant, though." Jackson assembled olives and pineapple and mandarin oranges onto the sauce-covered crust. "And I love catching it in a shot. It's thrilling."

"So why don't you sell your own work?"

Jackson shrugged. "I want the stable paycheck my job gives me."

He preheated the oven and added sun-dried tomatoes and crumbled bacon bits, covering it all with shredded mozzarella, asiago, and slices of chevre. To finish, he used fresh basil leaves from a plant growing on his counter. Once in the oven, he gestured for Al to follow him to the sofa so they could watch the movie.

Jackson sat close, resting his head on Al's shoulder. Al's body stiffened, Jackson figured he must be hungry and resisting out of politeness.

"Hungry?"

He grunted but didn't move.

"Don't worry, I won't let you go to sleep hungry." Jackson patted Al's thigh.

He knew the pizza, while it would still taste good, wouldn't actually feed a vampire, but if Al was willing to keep him company for the night, a little blood seemed a fair trade. Besides, Jackson enjoyed kisses to his throat and sort of enjoyed the strange, heady rush of blood flowing out of him when they fed—though it was always frightening, knowing if they didn't stop, he'd die.

They started the movie. Jackson scooted closer as they watched it. By slow degrees, Al relaxed, his fingers slipping up and down Jackson's arm. Jackson sighed. It'd been too long since he could relax beside someone without them trying to get down his pants.

When the timer chimed from the kitchen, Jackson was reluctant to get up. He didn't bother pausing the movie—he'd seen it three times already. While the pizza was cooling, Jackson checked his reflection in a small mirror hanging on the wall. He combed his fingers through the tangle of curls spiraling up from his head.

"You want a drink? I have vodka, rum, or sparkling water." He called into the living room.

"I'm good," Al replied.

Jackson sliced the pizza into eight slices, inhaling the warm, fresh aroma of bread and melted cheese. Even with store-bought crust, he could tell the pizza turned out perfect. He brought a plate out to Al, sitting beside him. Al blew on it, steam rising up just short of his lips, and then took a huge bite.

"Damn, you weren't kidding. This is amazing."

"I told you." Jackson took his own generous bite.

Al's dark eyes glazed over, his own jaw going slack as he watched Jackson eat. Al shook his head and returned his focus to his pizza. After eating, Jackson wrapped up the leftovers and went back to cuddling on the couch.

"This is nice," Jackson muttered, eyelids getting heavy.

"Y-yeah. It is..." A long, comfortable pause nestled between them. Then Al whispered, "My name is Alel. My real name. Al's a nickname."

"Alel," Jackson sighed, curling closer to Alel and closing his eyes. "You have a beautiful name."

"I guess. I shouldn't have told you."

"Don't worry." Jackson fumbled for Alel's hand, squeezing it. "I understand, so you don't have to fight it. Act natural around me, okay?"

"I can't," Alel whispered.

"It's okay. I don't mind. Better hurry, though, or I'll fall asleep." Jackson yawned, proving his point.

"I should go." Alel brought up Jackson's hand to his lips, kissing it. "Before I do something stupid."

"Don't go. You're still hungry."

"I'm starving."

Jackson squeezed Alel around the waist, waiting and waiting and waiting for the sting of teeth against his throat. He fell asleep waiting.

ALEL LAY ON a sofa with a human in his arms. He stared at the ceiling, trying to sort the strange feeling struggling in his chest. Desire rose from Jackson, hot as a fever, but it wasn't lust. Alel couldn't figure out *what* it was.

But it made him want to touch Jackson, badly. His charmed fingers ran up and down Jackson's warm-toned, tawny brown arms. To an outside observer, their skin would be the difference between dark amber and onyx, but truly it was wild buckwheat honey and kefir.

He dozed with Jackson, tired and lethargic from going a week without food, but ever since Sariel had asked him for a kiss, Alel couldn't force himself to have a one-night stand, no matter how many times he told himself he needed to eat. He was eager enough, cock hard and begging every time he passed someone in the streets, but no one stimulated his appetite.

Except Jackson. The human had a body made for the bedroom, hair a wiry, uneven halo that looked bed strewn, and his lips were thick and...plush, and—*oh fucking God*—those lips would be Alel's downfall. They were so broad and so plump, and when Jackson smiled, they revealed a flash of teeth with a gap in the center that made his grin adorable—irresistible. Alel wanted to taste him, taste him and glide his fingers over Jackson's warm skin. Jackson's mouth was so gorgeous, how could Alel not want to kiss him?

Alel huffed out an exasperated sigh, closed his eyes, and tried to sleep, but sleeping was something he usually only did after sex, so he lay in the quiet living room and listened to Jackson breathe. During the quietest part of night, when the traffic grew sparse and the smog hid the stars and before the sun came to force a new day onto people still weary from the previous twenty-four hours, Jackson shifted and moaned. He stretched, arching with the grace and beauty of a ballet dancer, and Alel's heart fucking raced at the sight.

Jackson scratched the little twists of curls growing from his scalp and gazed at Alel with sleepy, content brown eyes.

"You're still here?"

Alel nodded, watching Jackson with something paramount to awe.

"Why didn't you...you know?"

"You were asleep," Alel answered.

It was strange how Jackson almost seemed to know. But the glamour still hugged his form which meant he appeared human. He was startled from his thoughts when Jackson crawled into Alel's lap, leaning close and pressing their noses together.

"I appreciate you staying while I slept."

"Um..." Alel tried to swallow, but couldn't.

"It's almost dawn. You should probably go." Jackson planted a single kiss onto Alel's forehead.

Alel's breath hitched from the dry press of lips against his skin. He closed his eyes, inhaled the leftover scent of the cologne Jackson had worn the previous night. Then he blinked, confused with everything. Jackson slipped off his lap so he could stand.

"Alel?" Jackson asked, shifting his weight and rubbing his arm.

"Yeah?"

And *this* is when it should have happened. Jackson should have stepped close, slipped his hand down Alel's pants, toyed with his cock, led him toward the bedroom. The air was thick with energy. In any other circumstance Alel would already be slipping out of his clothes, but still, he couldn't sense any *lust*. It was something else, something confusing, something terrifying, and Alel backed away from Jackson toward the door.

"Want to come back next weekend?" Jackson stared at the TV. He didn't notice Alel's wide, panicked eyes or slow steps backward. "I had a lot of fun last night."

Alel froze in place, feeling *he* was the one being tempted. He stared at Jackson, searching for traces of fay or fox or any other manner of creature who'd have fun toying with a low-level incubus, and while it was true Jackson had the toasted, golden-brown eyes of a fox, he didn't seem to have any of the body language or mannerisms of one.

Jackson gave him a worried glance, and Alel realized he was taking too long to answer. Alel fumbled in his pocket, pulling out his cell phone and handing it to Jackson, who gave Alel a wide grin.

"Is that a yes?"

Alel couldn't bring himself to say the word, so he nodded instead. Were his hands sweating? Were the top points of his ears blushing? Why was he giddy? Alel wondered if *this* was why demons didn't cuddle or watch movies. He was dying.

Jackson typed his number into Alel's cell phone, pressing it back into Alel's hand and slipping close to peck his cheek.

"See you next week."

Alel turned, their mouths close. He licked his own lips, but he didn't dare... He didn't dare.

"Good night," he whispered and rushed out of the apartment.

The morning air nipped at his skin. A brisk shiver ran through him. *That* he understood, stimulus and reaction he understood; *Jackson* he didn't understand at all.

"Did you have fun?" A voice asked beside him.

Alel turned his head, seeing Sariel. He snarled and bared his teeth at the angel.

"Are you here to gloat?"

"I'm here to walk you home and to see how your date went."

"Don't call it a date. We don't know who's listening—and no, it wasn't fun because I didn't get laid."

"You haven't gotten laid all week."

"Because I want to fuck an angel." Alel flashed teeth as he faked a grin.

"We can hold hands." Sariel laced his fingers with Alel's. "I know you don't think it's as good, but angels hold hands all the time. It makes us happy."

"I don't want to be happy, I want to come," Alel whined, too desperate to be anything less than sincere. "This is your fault. You owe me. Aren't angels compassionate? Show me compassion and come back to my place. Otherwise I'll starve to death and it'll be your fault."

"I don't think you'll starve to death at all. I think hell lies, and you're miserable because of those lies." Sariel squeezed Alel's hand. "Notice you're not letting go?"

"I'm seducing you. You said angels hold hands, right? If this is what you do instead of fucking, then I'll try it."

"You know what else we do?" Sariel laughed, wrapping his arms around Alel and embracing him.

His stomach looped, and he started to shake a little. The angel's light washed over his skin. It was amazing, and it was horrible. Alel held his breath; it was too much. Suddenly he realized why demons didn't seduce angels.

"You're hurting me," Alel whimpered.

"You're lying," the angel said.

"You're scaring me." Alel smashed his teeth against his bottom lip.

"Oh." Sariel pulled away, looking empathetic. "That was the truth. I'm sorry."

"It's not fair." Alel spun and started marching to his own apartment.

His glamour flickered out, leaving him pale and scrawny, but he was too shaken and exhausted and hungry to sustain it. He dug his nails into his palms, blinking as the sun started to burn the gray from the sky, but the light hadn't reached the streets yet and Alel strolled in building-cast shadow.

"Alel!" The angel ran after him.

"Don't touch me anymore."

"I'm trying to be your friend. I'm trying to show you it's okay—not everything has to be carnal."

"*For you.* It doesn't have to be carnal *for you.* I'm a demon, not an angel, I can't just hold hands and be okay."

"I've *watched* you." Sariel continued to march beside him. "You hardly eat, you call humans by name, you touch their hair, you're tender even in bed."

"I'm going to bite you if you don't shut up," Alel snarled. The angel was calling him out on some dangerous habits, things that could get Alel pulled back to hell for a couple hundred years of re-education.

Sariel ruffled their wings, light flaring and settling around their body. When they reached Alel's apartment, he stood and glared at the angel, refusing to invite Sariel in unless it was for sex.

"There's nothing wrong with you!" The angel shouted in the hallway. "I don't care if you're an incubus! Stop forcing yourself! You're better than the other demons!"

"I'm not a pet project for you to convert!" Alel shouted back into the angel's face. "Go the fuck away!"

He opened his apartment door and slammed it in the angel's face. Alel paced the length of his living room. He knocked over the idol sitting on an end table and kicked his sofa until his foot throbbed. With a frustrated growl, Alel marched to his bedroom, wrapped himself up in a comforter, and slept most of the week.

Without a lover to feed off, he didn't have the energy to do much else.

Chapter Three

SATURDAY ARRIVED AND Alel decided he'd do something he hadn't done in over five thousand years—try. Jackson wasn't the type to spread his legs after drinking three beers at a party. If it took two, or even three dates to seduce him, the meal would be much more savory, a slow-simmered dish, *coq au vin,* pun intended.

Alel lay on his bed, fighting his way into a pair of black leather pants. He'd doused himself with a perfume given to him by an Egyptian noble over 4,000 years ago that smelled of water lilies, lotus flower, and cinnamon. He also put extra effort into his glamour, making sure his skin seemed oiled and his braids appeared to be freshly washed and conditioned.

He'd texted Jackson the previous day to work out details and arrived at his apartment after sundown. Jackson's eyes widened when he opened the door and saw Alel. He rested a hand on Alel's hips, pulling him in and giving him a brief kiss on the cheek.

"Wow, you look *amazing.*"

"So do you." Alel couldn't take his eyes off Jackson.

His skin demanded to be touched, licked, bitten. His hair demanded to be tugged, pulled, yanked. Alel wanted to slam him against the wall and kiss him—a thought he quickly edited to *fuck*—but the original image lingered in his mind. Alel imagined Jackson's fingers teasing Alel's cock while Jackson's tongue slipped into Alel's mouth. His groin reacted to the thought with a strong hitch upward. He swallowed a thick moan, but Jackson was already pulling away.

"I made steak, extra rare. It's resting right now but should be ready."

Alel followed Jackson into the dining nook adjacent to the kitchen. He had taper candles lit between their place settings and irises in a vase next to the candles. Alel reached out, touching the violet petal of an iris.

"Is it too much?" Jackson asked.

Alel glanced over his shoulder, noticing the strain in Jackson's voice. His expression was concerned, as if he'd overstepped a boundary.

"They're beautiful," Alel said.

Jackson's face broke into a grin making Alel want to kiss him even more.

"I get teased for being a hopeless romantic, but I like it, you know? Cheesy, cliché stuff is my jam. What's wrong with candlelit dinners and moonlit walks, and holding hands, and kissing with your eyes closed?"

Alel flushed at the thought of holding hands and kissing—eyes closed or open. He had thought a lot about holding hands since the other morning with Sariel. He hadn't minded it, and that's why it bothered him. Angels were backward creatures. If the stupid angel wanted to be his friend and hold his hand, Sariel should at least suck Alel off first. It was indecent otherwise.

"Alel? Are you okay?"

"I never thought about it," he said, "but I wouldn't mind trying it—walking at night and holding hands."

"We could, if you wanted to." Jackson toyed with the tongs in his hand. "Tonight after dinner maybe?"

"Yes," Alel's stomach flopped. It was oddly similar to the way a lover felt inside him.

"Really? Okay—okay, yeah. Let's hurry and eat so we can go. I made yours extra rare."

"My favorite." Which was true. Rare beef tasted so good sometimes Alel wished he could live off food like humans did for the excuse to eat it more.

"I figured." Jackson laughed at some joke Alel didn't get.

They ate the steak with a baked sweet potato and asparagus. The food was good, despite its uselessness to Alel.

"Where did you learn how to cook? Everything you make is amazing."

"I taught myself when I became vegan in high school. I studied every cookbook, cooking show, and YouTube video I could find."

"You were vegan?"

"Well, obviously not now, but for a long time, yeah. I still don't eat a lot of meat, but I figured tonight was sort of special, and I'd need the iron."

"Um, yeah," Alel muttered, not understanding why Jackson would need iron, but hoping it had something to do with sex.

"So what did you do all week?" Jackson asked as he cut into his food.

"Nothing much. I slept a lot."

"I'm sorry about last week, about falling asleep. I'll try to make it up to you tonight."

"Don't apologize," Alel said to his plate, his stomach tying into knots. "I had fun last week."

"Really?"

"Yes."

"You don't have to pretend."

"It was different." Alel forced himself to take another bite, stomach too twisted with nerves to want food inside it. "Usually I take what I need and go home, but I *did* have fun last week."

"Good, because I had fun too." Jackson stabbed at his asparagus.

Their conversation slipped into easier flowing topics. Vincent Price movies, and the Doors, and "Lord of the Rings" books. They had a lot in common, and two hours passed without Alel realizing until he noticed the candles were only stubs.

"Did you still want to walk?" Jackson asked as he cleared the plates from the table.

"Yes." Alel was even more excited about the thought than when he'd first agreed to it. It gave him an excuse to talk to Jackson a little longer.

They went outside and started down the street. The stars struggled against a world of traffic lights and skyscrapers, but the ones shining through the light pollution were beautiful.

"There's no moon tonight; so much for a moonlit walk." Jackson sighed.

"But there's you," Alel muttered. "And that's better than the moon."

"That's—"

"Stupid, so stupid." Alel cursed himself as he spoke out loud. "I shouldn't say such things."

"No, it was..." Jackson used their linked hands to pull Alel closer. Jackson brushed his free fingertips against Alel's cheek. "The nicest thing anyone's ever said to me on a date."

"Oh." Alel's lashes fluttered.

Jackson stared at Alel, whose mouth was a cute little confused O. They leaned a little closer, and Jackson almost kissed him, but Alel jumped when a nearby taxi honked at traffic. Jackson laughed and dragged him down the street.

"C'mon, I want to show you something."

"What?"

"It's a surprise."

They kept a decent pace for two blocks, Alel dizzy from hunger. When they stopped, Alel leaned against the bark of a tree. He looked around; they were surrounded by a patch of pines.

"It's a bike trail leading to a park," Jackson explained, "but if you stand here, it's easy to pretend you're out of the city."

"It's nice." Alel reached out and touched Jackson's cheek again. Jackson stepped closer, pressing their chests together.

"This is my favorite spot in town, so I wanted to share it with you."

"Do you prefer getting away from the city?" Alel asked.

"When I can. I don't mind living here, but camping is one of my favorite vacations."

"I've never gone."

"It's the best." Jackson's thumb creased the top ridge of Alel's cheekbones. "Fires and s'mores and sleeping bags under the stars."

"It does sound good."

Alel's vision spun. Jackson's chest rose and fell as he breathed. The faint scent of pine sap fought against the traffic fumes, and the streetlight filtering through the branches *could* be moonlight with a little imagination. It felt safe, private. He didn't think any other demons would accidentally catch them as they hid for a few minutes in their own little world of trees.

So, although he shouldn't, he shouldn't, fire and brimstone, *he shouldn't*, he leaned in and lightly touched his lips to the corner of Jackson's mouth. And, *oh fuck* was it a good feeling: tingling, and thrilling, and nerve-wracking all at once.

Jackson stared at Alel as if he wanted another kiss, perhaps a deeper, more sensual one, but Alel didn't have the nerve to break taboo twice.

"Did you want to walk more?" Jackson asked after a moment.

"Here's good." Alel pulled Jackson closer still. "Are you cold?"

"Not with you holding me."

"Good." Alel smiled.

They stood in silence with their chests pressed together. They listened to the traffic and night birds. Alel curled against Jackson, hiding his sight in the curve of Jackson's neck.

"This...feels good," Alel moaned, breathless, same as he would in the bedroom. His entire body shuddered in forbidden pleasure as he held Jackson for the sake of it instead of seduction.

"Really?" Jackson sucked in a quick breath.

"Yes."

"Hmmm, I'm glad." Jackson ran his fingers up and down Alel's chest. "Let's stay here for a few minutes longer."

Alel arched into Jackson's touch, thankful for the tree supporting his back. They stood wrapped together until Jackson finally pulled away.

"Want to go back to my place?"

"Yes," Alel couldn't hide the eager tone in his voice. Their moment in the trees tasted sweet, a popsicle, something he could only lick; he was desperate for something more substantial. Jackson lowered his eyes, giving him a flirtatious grin.

"Then let's hurry home."

They rushed back hand in hand, talking and laughing the entire way home. Once they crossed the threshold to Jackson's apartment, they kicked off their shoes next to the door and crashed side by side onto the couch.

"It's still early." He leaned up and ran the tip of his nose across Alel's cheek.

His lips brushed across Alel's face. The incubus gasped and allowed Jackson to move along his skin. Alel batted his eyes, trying to process the soft, sweet actions. People usually grabbed for his dick at this point, clothes usually scattered to the floor, so why was Jackson teasing Alel's temple with his bottom lip? Alel thought perhaps it was a strange fetish, or he told himself it was so he could justify how good it felt, but he couldn't sense any lust radiating from Jackson's skin—only a bizarre *other* feeling Alel didn't understand. It was similar to being fed grapes, sweet and juicy and plucked from a lover's fingers, not a meal in itself but a delightful experience.

Jackson dug his fingers into Alel's shoulders and shifted higher, baring his throat beneath Alel's lips. Alel lidded his eyes, lips parting. He could feel the warmth and life from Jackson's skin against his lips, although they weren't yet touching. Alel exhaled, and Jackson shuddered as breath washed over his skin. Alel's mouth watered as he hovered his lips above the curve of Jackson's throat.

"It's all right," Jackson whispered. "I know you want to. I can tell you're hungry."

It was true. He was so hungry, but he wanted his lips on Jackson's neck far more than a quick meal. Alel's face felt aflame; his lips tingled with want. To breach that forbidden barrier, to press his lips precariously against the delicate skin of Jackson's throat, the thoughts were driving Alel mad, mad, mad, mad, mad, *mad*.

To grab Jackson's hips, to plunge into the tightness of his asshole and thrust until he was spent, *those* would have been fine and savory thoughts, but that was *not* what Alel thought of. He would have loved to, afterward, but the thought throbbing in the forefront of his mind was simple, wickedly simple—drag his mouth up Jackson's throat. Taste his skin. Press his lips to flesh and savor Jackson's heartbeat against his tongue.

"Alel, you don't have to fight it. I already said it was okay, give into to what you want." Jackson crawled into Alel's lap, silently daring him to put his mouth on Jackson's skin.

"Oh, God," Alel moaned at Jackson's words, and as much as Alel wanted his cry to be blasphemy, it was far more a prayer of thanksgiving.

He was sinking, drowning in a current of *need*. His lips ghosted across the pulse point of Jackson's neck. Jackson sucked in a sharp breath, tensing as if expecting something much harsher. Alel reached up, cradling the back of Jackson's head with his right hand while holding his waist with his left hand. He leaned in again, giving Jackson's skin an experimental lick. He moaned, licking again, longer, slower. He ended with a wet, sloppy kiss. His lips were clumsy, inexperienced, but he struggled through the awkwardness as he experimented with his mouth against Jackson's throat.

Jackson sighed and hummed in pleasure, little vibrations tickling Alel's lips from the sound. His body relaxed a little with each new kiss against his throat, but then he pushed away and glared at Alel.

"Why won't you bite me?"

"Is biting what you're into?"

"I meant feed. Isn't that why you were at the party?"

"Y-yes, but how did you know?" Alel asked, suspicious.

"My skin tickles when I'm close to you, so you're obviously wearing a glamour. Why are you playing games with me? Drink my blood or go home."

"Your blood? But I don't—oh." Alel sat and stared up at Jackson, who was still in his lap. It was hard to think; his head spun from having free reign of Jackson's neck.

"What?" Jackson snapped, still frustrated from confusion.

"I'm not a vampire."

"Then why are you charmed?"

"I, um... I'm something else." He stood, his stomach threatening to purge itself of the steak. He licked his lips, remembering how good it had tasted despite the fact Alel couldn't absorb any real nutrition from it. "Maybe I should go."

"Wait a damn minute. You can't leave without an explanation. Undo the spell. I want to see what you really are."

"I'd rather not." Alel marched for the door.

Jackson ran in front is him, grabbing a camera hanging from a key hook near his door. He brought it up to his face.

Alel winced, holding out his hand to shield himself.

"Don't! I'm ugly!"

"What the fuck are you?" Jackson shouted, lowering, then raising the camera again.

Alel sighed, dropping the glamour and scratching his arms as the irritating magic left his skin. He couldn't face Jackson, so he stared at the floor.

"A demon. An incubus."

"Oh." Jackson looked crestfallen, leaning against the door and sliding to the floor. "Dammit. You're the exact opposite of what I wanted, and we got along so well too."

The words wounded Alel in a way a demon shouldn't hurt. Alel crossed his arms over his chest, holding his breath. Seconds later, he spat out a bitter retort.

"Well, excuse me. I didn't know you had a vampire fetish when *you* invited *me* over to your place."

"It's not a fetish. It's practical! Vampires don't have sex, only bloodlust. I wanted to have a nice night without getting molested."

"I have *never* taken an unwilling lover to bed!" Alel balled his hands into fists.

"I didn't mean to imply—I'm sorry if I was rude. I've had bad experiences with humans. I date vampires because they'll hang out for hours if I let them feed a little. It's nice, but if you're an incubus..." Jackson rubbed the bridge of his nose, face wrinkled with stress lines.

Alel dropped to the ground, knees hitting the tiled floor with a disappointing *thud*.

"Yeah...we feed off of sexual energy instead of blood. Is that so bad? Everyone wants sex."

"I don't. Well, I *do*, but I hardly ever want it. Kissing is great, and I don't mind a bit of fooling around, but when it comes to fucking..." He sighed. "See the problem?"

"Damn. Yeah, I see the problem."

Alel wondered why this bothered him when it shouldn't. It didn't happen often, but sometimes a human wasn't interested, and previously, he'd leave them be and find someone more eager to feed from. Hungry as he was, he flinched at the thought of more clubs, parties, and bars.

"I'm sorry, you seem great, but you'd starve to death around me."

"Doesn't matter." Alel lifted up his shirt, exposing white skin stretched over his ribcage. "I'm already half starved."

Jackson gasped. "Why? You're skin and bones."

"I don't know... Have you ever been on a road trip where you spend a few days eating out of drive-thrus and gas stations?"

"Yeah." Jackson nodded his head.

"That's how it feels—traveling and eating out of my car, and I'm sick of it. Nothing tastes good anymore. I'm hungry. I'm going crazy because I'm so hungry, but I don't want to *eat anything.*"

Alel dropped to Jackson's floor, spread eagle and staring at the ceiling. He couldn't deny his thoughts anymore. He craved *real food*, something homemade and not out of a greasy paper bag.

"I don't know what's wrong with me. None of the others seem to mind hand jobs in back alleys or one-night stands in hotels, but..." Alel frowned. He felt wrong and bruised inside, a circus freak on display. "This whole mess is the angel's fault."

"The...angel?"

"Yes. That asshole gave me the address to the party where we met. I'm not sure why I went."

Jackson laughed, pushing himself up and walking over to Alel. He covered his laughing mouth with one hand.

"What?"

"You said an angel gave you the address to a party? Who invites an angel to a party?"

"I think he stole the paper it was written on."

"I don't think an angel would steal anything." Jackson offered his other hand. Alel accepted, and Jackson pulled him to his feet. Jackson mussed Alel's hair. "You're short."

"Don't mess it." Alel fussed, stepping back. "I can't help being short. I don't eat enough."

"You have purple freckles." Jackson stepped close again into Alel's personal space. He brushed his fingertips across Alel's cheeks.

"Ugh, I should have never shown you my real body." Alel turned his face away.

"I think they're adorable. Your real body is cute; it's better than the glamour you were wearing."

"Liar," Alel hissed. "I look half dead."

Jackson cupped Alel's face and forced him to turn back so they faced each other again. He brushed the side of his thumb across Alel's freckled cheek.

"I'm sorry I can't give you what you need. I wish I could. Once, I tried to just do it for a guy, thinking maybe it wouldn't be so bad." Jackson shook his head. "But I ended up hating it, and I wasn't happy, and it was awkward afterward, so we broke up."

"It's fine." Alel clutched at Jackson's shirt. The fear of going back to a nightclub and finding Naberius made Alel's arms shake worse than when Sariel hugged him. He didn't blame Jackson, however. In fact, he envied Jackson for being able to tell someone no without going to bed hungry.

"I had so much fun the last two weekends; too bad incubi can't feed off making out and cuddling."

"We're not allowed to kiss," Alel mumbled, eyes squeezed shut as he tried to deny the world around him.

"Not allowed?"

"Lust forbid it when they created us."

"Your tree of knowledge between good and evil is *kissing*?"

"I never considered that." Alel laughed at the thought.

"But you kissed my neck?"

Alel's face burned. He pressed his lips together and refused to answer Jackson.

"You weren't supposed to, were you?"

Alel shook his head no.

"But I kept tempting you because I thought you wanted to bite me instead of kiss me."

"It was a reasonable misunderstanding. I should have figured it out when you invited me into the apartment and didn't put garlic on the pizza."

"Kinda makes me the talking snake, doesn't it?" Jackson stepped forward, forcing Alel to step back.

"I shouldn't discourage pride or blasphemy, but that's a rather lofty comparison." Alel kept stepping back as Jackson herded him away from the door.

Then Jackson shoved Alel. His breath caught in his throat as he fell, landing with a grunt against the sofa cushions. Jackson crawled over the sofa arm and Alel's legs. He straddled Alel on the couch and peered down with a smirk upturning the corner of his mouth. Jackson brought their lips close together, and if he was a snake, Alel was a sparrow paralyzed by Jackson's hypnotic gaze.

"I figured this is the least I can do after all the confusion I caused."

"What are you—"

Every nerve lit up in Alel's body at once. Lightning streaked through his groin and he bucked on reflex. Jackson molded their lips together. Alel squealed in delight as Jackson traced Alel's bottom lip with the tip of his tongue. Jackson cradled the back of Alel's head, holding him up while their lips moved. Alel opened his mouth and Jackson deepened their kisses, slipping his tongue into Alel's mouth. He muffled another squeak, reaching out with his own tongue and sliding it against Jackson's. After several minutes, Jackson pulled away, breathing heavily. Alel pulled at his shirt, trying to bring them close again.

"Don't stop, please."

"Nothing bad will happen, will it? If we do this?"

"Golden Rule of Hell—it's only wrong if you get caught, and Satan's not omnipresent," Alel said in a rush of desperation. In truth, hell had numerous spies, but he didn't care at the moment.

"Okay." Jackson grinned, indulging Alel with three more presses of his lips. "We're only making out, all right? I don't want to lead you on."

"Jackson! Kiss me, god dammit!" Alel begged, too caught up in the moment to worry about anything else. Both starvation and demonic treason were far-off concerns compared to the urge to drag his lips against Jackson's until there was no more breath left between them.

"Just setting boundaries." Jackson snorted, before smashing their mouths together and pulling another needful moan from Alel.

Alel tucked his tail between the couch cushions so his barbed tip didn't accidentally stab Jackson in a moment of excitement. He did his best to lay still and let Jackson take the lead, but occasionally, Alel's hips hitched out of reflex, pressing his hard cock against Jackson's body. Each time it happened, Alel whimpered from both the jolt shooting through his body and the unresolved ache of not being able to come. He'd never been so aroused in his six thousand years of existence.

Jackson dropped his lips to Alel's throat, nibbling and then sucking hard against the skin.

"Yes! Yes! God, please, yes!" Alel shouted to the ceiling and trembled as he damn near came in his zipped-up jeans.

Jackson pulled back with a loud, smacking sound, shifting his weight and making Alel cry out. Their kisses slowed, becoming deep and sensual. Alel's mind careened, drunk and giddy off the nectar of forbidden fruit.

Jackson's hair became an angelic halo as sunlight streamed in through the apartment windows. Squares of gold and orange painted the ceiling and the universe was so beautiful Alel broke their kiss to gasp in wonder and stare at Jackson's face. His lips were swollen and dark from friction, and his eyes glimmered in the morning light.

"I think," Alel whispered, reaching up and using his fingertips to tease Jackson's lips, "They only ever banned kissing because it's so wonderful they were afraid of it."

"No one's ever said anything that beautiful to me." Jackson rubbed an eye with a closed fist.

"Jackson?" Alel blinked, frowning and confused despite the lingering high of the past hour. "Are you crying?"

"Kinda." Jackson sniffed, wiping away a single tear with his opposite hand. "How fucked up is my life when every human I've ever dated tries to guilt-trip their way into my pants, but the *literal-fucking-sex-demon* doesn't?"

"I don't know, how fucked up is my life? I'm a literal-fucking-sex-demon, but I'd rather come here next week and make out instead of finding someone who'd let me into their pants?"

"Won't you starve?"

"I..." Alel paused, raising up on his elbows. "I feel okay, actually. A little drunk, but I'm not as hungry as I thought I'd be."

"But you're still hungry?"

"I'm always hungry." Alel snorted, avoiding Jackson's eyes.

"We stayed up all night." Jackson fidgeted with the hem of his shirt. The last hour was more amazing than anything he could remember in his life, but they still wore their clothes.

"I can go home." Alel waited for Jackson to stand so he could sit up.

"Yeah, but, if you wanted to take a nap first I could make up the couch? Fix pancakes before you go? You can eat food, right? I mean, you've been eating food, but it's not going to make you throw up or anything?"

"Eating's fun, but it's empty calories, like drinking beer. I can't live off it."

"D-do you *want* to stay and eat pancakes with me?"

"Sure, if you don't mind," Alel rambled, out of his element. His face burned. "Pancakes sound good."

"It would be nice if you stayed."

"I've never stayed overnight, especially on the couch." Alel grinned and scratched behind one of his horns. "This feels a bit like skydiving to me."

"Would you ever try skydiving?" Jackson stood up, his expression excited. "Because I've always wanted to!"

"You know, I *can* fly." Alel spread out his wings. Light from the windows struck the leathery underside of his wings, revealing a webwork of veins and capillaries.

"I wondered, but I thought it rude to ask." Jackson reached out his hand. "Can I touch them?"

"I wouldn't mind," Alel snapped his wings against his back again, flushing, "but they're an erogenous zone, my tail too."

"Oh!" Jackson pulled his hand back in. "Sorry."

"I thought I should tell you."

"Yes. Thank you."

"Um..." Alel looked around the room. "My horns aren't as sensitive. You could touch those."

Jackson bit his bottom lip. He reached out and thumbed up the side of one of the small, black horns rising from Alel's head.

"How does it feel? When I touch them?"

Alel toyed with Jackson's curls. "Same as you playing with my hair."

"Feels nice." Jackson stepped closer, reaching up with his other hand to comb through Alel's shaggy mess of hair.

A strange sort of gravity pulled Alel in. He didn't understand until his lips ghosted over Jackson's mouth. They stood and made soft passes over each other's lips until some unspoken cue made them step back and pull their hands away from each other's hair.

"I'll get some blankets." Jackson disappeared and returned with arms full of sheets and pillows and an old quilt.

"Thanks," Alel stared as Jackson made up the couch into a passable bed.

"I guess this is good night." Jackson plucked one last kiss from Alel's lips and retreated to his bedroom, leaving Alel to drop back to the sofa in a daze.

Chapter Four

JACKSON WOKE UP over an hour past noon. He yawned and stayed beneath the covers for a few extra minutes. His lips burned from his night with Alel, so Jackson licked them to cool them. It'd been a long time since he could truly relax and kiss someone without the omnipresent, unspoken expectation of sexual progression.

Jackson held his breath and jumped out of bed, sighing as he stood. He still didn't know what he was going to do with Alel. He enjoyed Alel's company so much the thought of not talking to him already hurt, but he couldn't let Alel starve. How much sex did an incubus need? Probably more than Jackson ever wanted to have, even if they did get close enough to where he wanted to have it at all. So then, should he let Alel feed on his own while dating Jackson? Jackson wrinkled his face with revulsion. The idea of his boyfriend going off for random sex with strangers soured Jackson's stomach.

As it stood, they seemed star-crossed and hopeless.

But Alel said he wanted to come back next weekend; the idea appealed to Jackson. He took a quick shower and changed into jeans and an old, baggy, comfortable-as-a-hammock-in-May T-shirt. He wandered into the living room. Alel lay rolled up in his blanket, shaggy hair and horns and the top half of his face the only bits of him exposed to the open air.

Jackson smiled, peering down at Alel's face. He knelt beside him, brushing his fingers on the top curves of Alel's cheeks and noticing how dark the circles beneath his eyes were. Jackson's lips drooped, the smile gone.

"Is breakfast ready?" Alel asked, stirring into consciousness from Jackson's light touch.

"I'm about to start cooking now."

Alel yawned, untangling himself from his cocoon and glancing at Jackson with a smile. Jackson sighed and went into the kitchen. Alel followed him, sitting on a stool near the island counter.

"What's wrong?"

"You know I'm not planning on sleeping with you, right?"

Alel scratched above his left eyebrow. "Yeah, you made that rather clear. Why? Did I say something lurid in my sleep? I don't remember dreaming."

"What? No." Jackson couldn't help a slight chuckle. "Do you talk in your sleep?"

"I don't know. I could."

"Well, you weren't when I came to wake you. But...you seemed tired and hungry."

"Would you feel more comfortable if I wore my glamour?"

"No, you're better as you are."

"Once, a few hundred years ago in Europe, an incubus named Naberius dragged me to a nunnery. He pulled me into this room, and waiting for us there, were these three gorgeous girls."

Jackson pulled a sour face as he mixed batter for the pancakes and heated the skillet.

"They had summoned Naberius, if you're making that face because you think we were preying on them. We only tempt humans—we don't make them do anything they don't already want to do. In this case, each of those girls had been sent to the nunnery by their rich, noble fathers. These girls wanted to have a wild night before they were forced to take vows of abstinence."

"That's not why I was frowning." Jackson ladled the first batch of hotcakes onto the skillet. "I just don't find women attractive, neither romantically, nor aesthetically."

"Ah, I thought you disapproved of the fact we were defiling soon-to-be-nuns. I have to admit, they tasted like syrup because they were so eager, but the Mother Superior caught us and used holy water to paralyze us. Naberius escaped—he eats as much as a linebacker, and he's as strong as one—but I was trapped."

"What'd they do?"

"Ever read 'The Cask of Amontillado'?"

"You are fucking kidding me. They walled you up in a catacomb?"

"Yes. Beneath a church even. It was painful to be walled within holy ground, and lonely, and it took over a decade until Naberius found me and carried me to the nearest farm where a hired hand helped give me enough strength to stand again. Do you understand what I'm saying?"

"Your friend's an asshole?"

"Well, he is, but demons can't be kind to each other. We'd be tortured for it. He... looks after me as best he can. He took me with him to make sure I was eating, and going to a party was only an excuse to rescue me."

"I'm sorry. Being a demon sounds rough."

"It's fine." Alel sighed. "Point is, I went without food for over ten years and didn't die."

"Oh." Jackson flipped the pancakes. The rich, warm smell of them filled the kitchen.

"You're worried, right? You don't want to get attached and then have me leave because I'm hungry, or sneak meals behind your back, and—it's true, this *is* stupid—I *need* sex to survive, but..." The stool scraped against the floor as Alel stood. He stared at Jackson, eyes huge and glassy. "You were a vegan, right? Why?"

"Why do we keep dogs as pets but eat cows? Why do we factory farm? None of it seemed right. Even now I mostly stick to fish." Jackson shrugged, scooping pancakes onto a serving platter and starting a new batch.

"I understand. I don't want factory-farmed lovers, and I'm so sick of Naberius telling me not to name the food." Alel smacked the counter with his palm. "Dammit, how am I supposed to enjoy myself if I have to fuck them without even knowing their names?" He dropped back to the stool, curling his face into the cradle of his arms.

"Alel?" Jackson stepped away from the skillet long enough to stroke the demon's hair.

Alel looked up at Jackson, eyes desperate and pleading.

"I'm made wrong, somehow. I was created to tempt people to carnal sin. To fuck, and drink, and lure others to do the same, but—" he squeezed his eyes shut, shaking his head. "I want sex. I want it all the time! At least, I'm aroused all the time? But—" he opened his eyes again. "Last night...was closer to what I really want. Closer than anything I've ever experienced in thousands of years. If *you* don't want to see me again, I understand, but—"

Jackson pulled himself onto the island counter and dragged himself over to where Alel sat. He sucked on Alel's lower lip for a full ten seconds before using his tongue. They didn't stop until he smelled the pancakes near burning. He rushed to his spot in front of the stove.

ALEL KISSED JACKSON goodbye. He tasted of butter and syrup, and Alel licked the flavor off Jackson's lips.

"Next week?" he asked once Jackson pulled away.

"Yup, and you don't have to wait until sundown now that I know you're not a vampire."

They both laughed and Alel walked out the door, waiting until Jackson closed it to slip the glamour back over his skin. Alel walked home lost in a daydream, everything around him invisible except the sidewalk. His fingers brushed over his lips every few minutes.

"So everything worked out well, yeah?"

"Go away, Sariel. I'm still mad at you."

"I'm sorry I hugged you. I know this is a lot for you to take in."

Alel snorted.

"Okay. I'll leave you alone. I'm sorry, Alel."

"Sariel?" Alel stopped and turned toward the angel.

"Yes?" The angel asked.

Alel hovered his hands an inch above Sariel's billowy, ivory-colored wings.

"Angels hold hands and they hold each other, but what if you're extra fond of someone? Ever rub your fingers through another angel's wings?"

"A-Alel, w-what are you doing? You can't touch my— we're on the street! It's not proper!" Sariel flushed.

"At least I know how to seduce an angel now." Alel laughed.

"What's so funny?" Sariel's brilliant pink complexion reminded Alel of dawn.

"Would you have let me? Had we been inside and not on the street?"

"I-I'd be tempted...but afraid. We're not supposed to do it."

"Your hug was the same for me, by the way. It was nice but...frightening." He took Sariel's hand and led him down the street.

"Are you dragging me back to your place?"

"Your curiosity smells like freshly made churros."

"Well I couldn't help *thinking* about it. I *do* wonder, how it feels. I've never tried it."

"Then I suppose demons aren't much different from angels after all. We just have different rules."

"You didn't answer my question. Are you taking me to your apartment?"

"Yes, but not for wing play, I'm afraid. I want to talk. I...I don't know who else to talk to about...things."

"All right." Sariel sighed. "I guess I'm your guardian angel too now."

"You ought to be. This is your fault, and if we get caught walking down the street, holding hands, we're both going to be in trouble."

"But aren't you happier now?"

"Happy? Stupid, idiot angel. Everything about this is awful. It was hard to eat before, but now it's impossible. No one but Jackson looks appetizing." He stopped and turned and dragged his fingers along Sariel's cheek. "Not even you. What a shame."

"It's not a shame; it's good," the angel said. "It means you care enough about Jackson not to hurt him."

"But this can't *possibly* work." Alel reached his apartment. This time he held the door open for Sariel to step inside.

"You have so many paintings of naked people." The angel's eyes darted across the walls.

"I love naked people. Admiring them...touching them..."

"Kissing them?"

"Kissing Jackson. Were you watching? Are angels voyeurs?"

"I only peeked in for a moment to make sure he was okay—it just happened to be during a very exciting moment."

Alel undid his glamour and dropped onto his sofa. The springs creaked against his weight, and he stared at the ceiling.

"Don't look so distressed." The angel sat beside him, patting his thigh. "It will all work out for the best."

"Your foolish, optimistic faith doesn't reassure me in the slightest."

"You do look awful." Sariel tilted Alel's chin to get a better view of him.

"Thanks."

"But you were worse last week."

"I don't see how that's possible."

"Your skin was ashen; now it has a glow."

"Sure." Alel snorted and turned away. "I don't know why I let you in. You're not any help."

"I think you're lonely, but I don't mind keeping you company for a few hours."

Alel frowned as he picked away bits of mangled cuticle with his thumbnails. His gaze jumped to Sariel.

"So what, um, should I do? I mean, next weekend when I see Jackson again. I've never dated. The hand-holding thing, right? And he eats because he's human, but where should we go?"

"Go bowling."

"Bowling?"

"Yeah. It'll be fun, and when you're finished, get pizza."

"No way." Alel's face flushed. "He makes his own. Takeout doesn't compare."

"Oh, I forgot. How about burgers?"

"He doesn't eat a lot of meat."

"Alel, I don't think you need me at all. You already know him better than I do." Sariel laughed.

"What good are you as a guardian angel if you don't even know what he eats or does?"

"I'm an angel, not a babysitter. The only reason I've been keeping an extra eye on him lately is because he's been depressed." Sariel's face twisted with concern. "I didn't want a real demon noticing him. I thought maybe with you—well, I can't interfere, but if things work out on their own, then all the better, right?"

"Fuck you. I am a real demon." Alel glared at the angel. "I'm shitty at it, but that doesn't change who I am."

"I wasn't trying to be rude. I meant I didn't want one of Sloth or Envy or Wrath's demons finding him. You know they love attacking humans when they're emotionally vulnerable."

"What's wrong with him?" Alel asked, his fidgeting migrating from his fingers to a loose thread poking out from the arm of the sofa. "Why would he be depressed? He seemed fine to me."

"He was never good at making friends, and anyone he dates ends up hurting him." Sariel glared. "Don't you dare ever hurt him."

Alel returned the scowl. "I'm the one risking starvation."

"Do you truly believe you'll starve?"

"Won't I?"

"I wasn't lying. You look better than before. You have a glow about you."

"Do angels eat food?"

"No?"

"I have chips."

"No, thank you?"

"I'm getting some." Alel stood up and went to his kitchen, returning with a bag of barbeque chips.

He grabbed the remote and put on the first show he saw. Alel shoved two chips into his mouth before tilting the bag into Sariel's direction.

"Eat one."

"I—"

"You owe me, for the hug."

"Fine." Sariel snatched a single chip and crammed the entire thing into their mouth. The angel's expression changed from perturbed to surprised. "Oh no. It's good. I was hoping it wouldn't be."

"I know the feeling." Alel snorted even as Sariel reached their hand back into the bag.

JACKSON WINCED WHEN he saw Alel. "Do you have to wear the glamour?"

"You said you wanted to go bowling with me."

"Yeah, *with you.*"

"I can't walk around town as an incubus. People would scream."

"Let them scream. I'm not ashamed to be seen with you." Jackson grabbed Alel's hand and gave it a defensive squeeze.

"Nice to hear, but I'm still going on this date incognito." Alel smiled despite himself, leaning forward and nuzzling against Jackson's untamed hair.

"It's your choice, but it pisses me off that you have to hide behind a glamour."

"I promise to take it off the moment we come back."

"Deal." Jackson followed him out the apartment.

The bowling alley was a new experience to Alel. In a way, it reminded him of a club, the loud music, the crowds, and the scent of human pheromones clinging to the air as thick as the smell of the fried food coming from the snack bar. The crash of bowling balls into pins was different, however, and Jackson shoved the ugliest pair of shoes Alel had ever seen against his chest.

"Do I have to?" He held the shoes away from him as if they'd been blessed by the Pope himself.

"Everyone wears these."

It was true, so Alel gave in and followed Jackson. The fluorescent lights gleamed against the waxed lanes. Alel noticed arrows marking the floor but didn't understand what they were for. The shoes on his feet were flimsy as paper.

"Do you think you can manage a ten-pound ball?"

"Usually the balls I handle are much smaller." Alel laughed.

"I don't recommend trying to fit this one in your mouth." Jackson poked Alel's shoulder before disappearing and returning with a marbled green ball.

"What do I do with it?"

"Seriously?" Jackson asked.

"I told you I've never played."

"Okay, come here." Jackson sat in front of a panel.

Alel stood beside him, but Jackson pulled him onto the edge of the seat, wrapping his arm around Alel's waist to keep him in place. Alel held his breath, stifling a grunt as Jackson's arm brushed against his side. Their pressed bodies were warm against each other. It reminded Alel of the moment before sex, when one fumbled with zippers and buttons, tension and clothing and—

"Pay attention."

"I want to kiss you," Alel whispered against Jackson's ear.

"Enter your name." Jackson gave him a little squeeze.

Alel blinked and stared at the monitor above them. It wanted the name of player two. He used the keyboard to type in Al and hit enter.

"Okay, I'll go first so you can watch me." Jackson stood, grabbed a ball, and went to the front of the lane.

"How am I supposed to pay attention when your ass looks so great in those jeans?"

Jackson winked and then focused on the pins. The game seemed easy enough. Jackson drew his arm back and swung forward, releasing the ball onto the gleaming lane. The ball spun and curved, veering back to the pins at the last moment and scattering them.

"I should probably warn you I was in a league as a kid, so…"

"So this is going to be a massacre." Alel took his green bowling ball. The weight pulled at his arm and wrist. The glamour gave his arms beautiful curves, but his real arms were twigs.

He stood at the line painted on the lane and chucked the ball for all he was worth. It thumped against the polished wood and made a slow, lazy line straight for the gutter. Alel crossed his arms, blushing out of fury as the ball took its time to get to the end.

"You get one more shot," Jackson said. "Here, let me help you."

As soon as Alel's ball returned, he went back to the front of the lane. Jackson showed him where to place his feet.

"Keep your wrist straight."

"It's heavy."

"Want a lighter ball?"

"No," Alel snapped. He'd already noticed Jackson used a fourteen-pound ball and didn't want to go any lower.

"I don't suppose hitting the gym would help you any, would it?"

"No." Alel sighed, frustrated.

Sex would help. Naberius had biceps thick as kegs, but Alel kept his mouth shut and his eyes on the pins ahead. He didn't want to say anything because he didn't want Jackson guilty about something neither of them could help. He threw the ball again and watched it roll down the lane. It meandered back toward the gutter and Alel held his breath as he willed the ball back to the center. Telekinesis wasn't in his skill set, however, so the ball continued to balance on the edge, nicking a single pin before it fell over.

"It's an improvement," Jackson said.

"One fucking point. You have ten."

"Yeah, actually I'll have more depending on my next turn."

"Really?"

"Yeah, you can get a score of 300."

"I suck." Alel groaned.

"It's your first game!" Jackson stole a quick kiss to Alel's forehead before grabbing his ball for his next turn.

Alel rubbed his forehead. He still wasn't quite used to the tingle of a kiss against his skin. Jackson made another strike and Alel grimaced. During his turn, he rolled the ball in the center, straight as he could. He managed to topple three pins.

"Getting better." Jackson held out a bright blue container to Alel.

"Poison to put me out of my misery?"

"Jello shot. I bought three for each of us because it's one-dollar happy-hour."

He usually didn't drink but figured a few wouldn't hurt. If the bright blue Jello had alcohol, he couldn't taste it. He rolled his ball again, but it went right for the small gap he'd already cleared on his first throw. Jackson only knocked over nine pins during the third frame. He still managed over two hundred while Alel bowled a forty-four.

"At least your score isn't perfect. My ego's suffering enough as it is. Want another game?" Alel asked.

"We can go, if you want." Jackson gave him a worried glance.

"No, I'm having fun. Well, it's fun watching you play."

"Really?" Jackson gave him a bashful smile, and suddenly leaving was the last thing Alel wanted to do.

"Go get some snacks, and I'll buy two more games."

They separated and met back at their lane. Jackson shoved a French fry into Alel's mouth the moment he returned. Alel ate it and opened his mouth for a second one.

"Lazy," Jackson scolded as he popped a second fry into Alel's mouth.

"You spoiled me when you fed me the first one."

Jackson replied by feeding him a third time. Alel had done this before, in the houses of nobles while trying to seduce young girls into bed, but he never had his heart fluttered because of it, or his face flushed, or his palms beaded with fine, tiny sweat droplets. Never did he yearn for the next bite or the accidental brush of Jackson's finger against his bottom lip.

"You told me you had a mother," Jackson said between frames.

"Lust is more my creator than a parent," Alel answered. "There's Satan and the original fallen angels, and then the Seven Sins appeared and created lesser demons."

"I bet family reunions are hell."

Alel almost dropped his ball when he got the pun. He managed to upturn seven pins and was pleased with himself.

"Can you actually play the violin?" Jackson asked as he stood for his turn.

"Yeah. I learned a few hundred years ago. It's amazing how lazy I've been since the Internet came out."

"Will you play for me? Maybe next week? I haven't been to your house yet."

"Yes, I'd love to see you again." Jackson's suggestion warmed Alel's stomach like a shot of whiskey.

"You're blushing. I can see it through the glamour." Jackson giggled and brushed his thumb along the crown of Alel's cheek, which only made his face warmer.

"I can't help it."

"This is the last game, right?" Jackson grinned. "Let's finish it up so we can go back to my place for coffee."

"This is the first time someone's ever invited me up for coffee and I've expected actual coffee."

"Oh, sorry." Jackson rubbed his arm.

"If it's as good as the pizza you made, I have no complaints." Alel winked and went on to roll a gutter ball, too busy thinking about coffee to throw the ball straight.

And it was good coffee, Alel decided an hour later as he sat in Jackson's kitchen. Jackson served it black, but it tasted of cinnamon.

Chapter Five

ALEL KNOCKED ON Jackson's door and then paced in front. It was only Wednesday, but Jackson had texted he wouldn't mind watching a movie before their Saturday date because he missed Alel. Alel had been pined for, lusted after, and coveted, but he did not think he'd ever been *missed* by someone, and it was a warm, comforting experience, like sipping creamy tomato bisque.

The door opened and Alel threw his arms around Jackson, unable to stop himself.

"Hi." Jackson squeezed him back and pulled him through the doorway.

Their mouths caught up together, and Alel sighed through his nose as he held Jackson's waist. They'd only kissed goodbye the previous night: long, lingering kisses tasting of coffee and cinnamon. They weren't enough, *not nearly enough* for a half-starved incubus newly learning all the glorious forbidden taboos of human affection.

"*House on Haunted Hill*?" Jackson asked when he pulled away.

"You know I'm always up for anything Price."

"Sit. I'll go grab the popcorn out of the microwave."

Jackson swaddled them in a fleece throw and nestled the bag of popcorn between their legs. The lights from the television winked across the room and played tricks on Jackson's face. Alel couldn't take his eyes off Jackson. The curve of his cheeks, the jut of his chin, Jackson was beautiful, but it was more than his appearance, it was *because he was Jackson*. It was all the little details hiding beneath the skin, and Alel wanted to undress everything about Jackson, layer by layer, in the world's slowest striptease.

"What?" Jackson noticed Alel staring and smiled.

"You're more interesting than the movie."

"You shameless flirt."

Alel's tail started to flick beneath the cover, excited. He stuffed it into the couch cushions to hide the reaction.

"Don't hide it. It's cute," Jackson said.

"It's also sharp."

"Only the end. I bet I could make a cap for it."

The thought of Jackson touching his tail, even to blunt the barb at the end, sent a shiver up Alel's spine.

"Cold?" Jackson asked when he noticed.

"No," Alel exhaled. "I-I'm fine."

"Oh." Jackson turned and stared at Alel for a long time. "You're hungry."

"I'm always hungry. I'm basically a cat." Alel forced a chuckle out of his mouth, but it sounded breathless and wanton.

Jackson swung himself into Alel's lap, leaning forward. "Your eyes are huge and your lips are plump and your hair is shinier than usual. It's almost as if you're wearing a glamour of your own image, only I can't feel any magic coming from you."

"You hate when I wear glamours." Alel's voice sounded small, his throat constricted. Jackson was *just right* in his lap and leaning close enough for his breath to tickle Alel's cheek.

"I know. That means it's you—it's how you look right now. You must be extra hungry."

"I uh, what I mean is, um, it'd be nice if you kissed me."

"Is that all you want? A kiss?" Jackson cooed, ghosting his lips across Alel's.

The demon whimpered. His lips parted to beg for more. Jackson teased the corner of his mouth and pulled at Alel's bottom lip. Their tongues reached out and slid together. Alel tilted his head, giving Jackson a silent cue to deepen the kiss. Jackson's fingers reached up. They stroked his horns and combed his hair, and Alel sank into the sensation of being kissed over and over. It was cucumber sushi wrapped in nori. It was salmon sashimi curled up inside a rose of pickled ginger. It was fresh steamed edamame and green tea and dango dusted with sweetened black sesame.

"Oh my god, you taste so good," Alel moaned as Jackson teased the corner of his mouth again. "Jackson...please, more." He gasped and tilted his head back to expose his throat.

Jackson seized the invitation and sucked until Alel's skin bruised beneath Jackson's lips. He rolled his tongue up Alel's throat and it was roe sushi and white tail sashimi and Alel grew bold enough to slip his hands up Jackson's shirt. He kept them tracing up and down Jackson's flat stomach, nothing too erotic, but sensual and admiring. Jackson's left hand tugged at Alel's hair while his right hand held his cheek. He mashed their lips together, quicker than before and a little sloppy, and it was all Alel could do to breathe.

A loud noise made them both jerk and turn toward the TV screen. The title menu played on a short, annoying loop of sound. They'd kissed through the rest of the movie and credits without noticing.

"Damnit," Jackson growled. "It's late, and I have a shoot tomorrow."

"Sorry." Alel wiped his mouth.

His lips seared from the friction of each kiss, but he savored the burning, raw sensation. The only thing missing was release, the dessert declaring the meal finished. Alel's balls screamed for it, but he'd do it all over again if he could, despite his aching groin, and he hoped to get the chance Saturday.

"Don't be sorry." Jackson grabbed his hand and kissed it. "I wanted to see you, and I wish we had a little extra time to kiss a bit more."

"Me too." Alel leaned forward, placing a soft, yearning kiss on Jackson's neck. "I'll be waiting for Saturday."

Jackson gasped at the kiss, and Alel experimented with a few more presses of his lips to Jackson's skin. Each one won a gasp from Jackson's mouth. He pulled away and kissed Jackson's forehead.

"Good night, Alel." Jackson kissed both of Alel's horns.

"Good night," Alel forced himself to leave so Jackson could get some sleep.

"WHAT ARE WE doing?" It was Friday night and Sariel sat in an incubus's kitchen eating potato chips and staring at the bowls and cups scattered across the counter.

Alel's phone sat on the counter half hidden by a bag of flour. Nina Simone sang from the phone speakers. One wouldn't think the kitchen belonged to a demon. It seemed wrong for a demon to have fruit-shaped magnets spread across an avocado-green refrigerator. The ceramic cats didn't help, either, nor did the old, dented kettle that had seen more than its fair share of tea bags and yet was polished to a bright gleam, obviously well-loved by Alel. It was an old grandmother's kitchen, not a demon's.

"Jackson always cooks for me, so I'm learning how to make chocolate chip cookies for him."

"How sweet."

"The other night...holy goddamn shit, Sariel, it was amazing."

"Was it the same as having sex? Were you feeding?" Sariel wrinkled their nose at the profanity but didn't mention it because they were more curious about what Alel was saying.

"No, you idiot angel. It was *nothing* like sex. Sex is chugging a bottle of Karo syrup or cramming stale cookies into your mouth. This was...texture, and flavor, and depth. It was being hand fed from a sushi boat. It was a feast. It was...it was fucking amazing."

"See, I told you—hell lies. You can feed off passion and affection as much as you did lust."

"If you had been wrong, I'd be dying right now."

"I had faith."

"Oh shut up and cream this butter and sugar while I get the other ingredients."

"How?"

"You're hopeless. You need to spend less time in the clouds and more time in the real world with the rest of us." Alel added the sugar and butter together and showed Sariel how to use the hand mixer.

"I'm an angel. I belong in the clouds." Sariel turned on the mixer and waited for the sugar and butter to lighten in color and fluff up. "Is this done?"

Alel leaned over and nodded.

"What's next?"

"Damn, I forgot to preheat the oven." He spoke to himself as he adjusted the oven dials. Alel turned around. "We add a tablespoon of vanilla, a teaspoon of baking soda, and a pinch of salt." As Alel said each item, he measured it and added it to the bowl.

"But how do you know?"

"I looked up a recipe on my phone. You really are hopeless." Alel opened up two bags of chocolate chips: white chocolate and dark chocolate.

"I suppose." Sariel grabbed Alel's cell phone to read the cookie recipe as Alel added flour one cup at a time.

"Hey, don't grab my phone. I could have naked pictures on there."

"Somehow I doubt it."

Alel snatched his phone back. "I *could* though. That's the point. Here, open wide so I can shove this in and see if I can make an angel moan."

Sariel rolled their eyes but humored Alel and opened their mouth. Alel crammed far too much cookie dough into Sariel's mouth, but they did moan.

Alel laughed and held the counter with both hands.

"Shut up." Sariel blushed. "I can't help it, dammit, you keep feeding me and food is delicious."

"You cursed too. Glad to see I'm not an utter failure as a demon."

"I hang out with you too much—so did you make extra for us or is this all for Jackson?" Sariel grabbed the wooden spoon and stole another scoop from the bowl.

"I made a double batch." Alel pulled the spoon out of Sariel's hand and snatched a quick bite before handing it back.

Sariel sighed and rested their cheek in their palm as they licked dough off the wooden spoon. "Can you imagine what one of the archangels would do if they saw us sitting in the kitchen eating cookie dough?"

"I'd imagine they'd kill me and lecture you until you wished you were dead." Alel fetched a metal spoon from a drawer and started spacing out balls onto the baking sheet.

"But I hate it. Alel, I hate it. *This is fun.* Why can't more angels and demons hang out together? We'll teach you to hold hands, and you can teach us to curse. We'll teach you to hug, and you can teach us how to bake cookies, and we'll all have a lovely time."

"Yes, and the war plaguing both sides since the dawn of mankind will be resolved." Alel snapped his fingers. "Simple as baking cookies."

"Why not? When's the last time you honestly felt different from a human? We've been here so long that we identify with *them* more than with our own kind."

Alel watched Sariel. The swing music blasting from Alel's phone prevented silence in the room, but neither spoke.

"I'm sorry. I shouldn't have said anything. It was stupid." Sariel looked away.

"No, you're right." He leaned forward, whispering. "You think some of the others feel the same?"

"I think a lot do, the angels at least. What about the demons?"

"It's hard to tell. We all lie so much." Alel pulled a face but then cheered up when Sariel offered him another bite from the wooden spoon.

JACKSON SAT ON Alel's couch, in awe of the demon as he played the violin. The bow trembled against the strings and pulled sharp, crisp notes from the instrument. Alel's tail flicked from side to side as he played, and his wings were spread out into the air. Light caught the black scales and tiny dark rainbows flashed across them.

Jackson bit his lower lip. He wanted to touch Alel's wings. He knew they were sensitive, but they were so beautiful. Jackson wanted to slide his fingers against the metallic turquoise, lime, and coral, which shifted depending on where the light struck. The song ended; the last note rang in the air.

"You're amazing." Jackson clapped his hands until they stung.

"Hundreds of years of practice." Alel stared at the floor, bashful and adorable.

"Will you play something else?"

A mischievous smile lit up Alel's face as he set his bow back against the string. Jackson scrunched up his face in delight when he recognized "The Devil Went Down to Georgia." He followed it with "Sympathy for the Devil." Jackson gave him a one-man standing ovation when he finished.

"Thanks," Alel muttered.

"Next time I'll bring roses to throw at your feet."

Alel stowed the violin in its case and afterward jumped into Jackson's arms. He was short and scrawny and easy to hold. They both laughed and rubbed noses. The light presses turned into soft nuzzling, and Jackson squeezed Alel more tightly.

"I'm glad you enjoyed the music," Alel said.

"I've never been serenaded." Jackson laughed, pressing little kisses into the side of Alel's neck and enjoying how they made the incubus shiver.

Alel grew heavy in Jackson's arms over time. He tried to readjust but was afraid of accidentally grabbing Alel's tail or wings, so he set him down. He kissed Alel's right horn and then his forehead.

"I'm a little hungry. Would it be okay if I ordered a pizza?"

"I bought cold cuts for sandwiches, and I baked cookies."

"Really? You baked cookies?"

"Sariel helped, but they were pretty useless—angels often are."

"Is it normal for demons and angels to hang out together?" Jackson asked.

"We've started an unofficial resistance movement. I'm going to teach Sariel how to play Mortal Kombat, and Sariel's going to—" Alel froze, blushing.

Jackson raised an eyebrow to question him.

"Um, I asked Sariel to give me a few ideas, a-about things humans do that aren't, y'know, sexual." Alel wrung his hands together. "Because I want to try them with you."

"What sort of ideas did Sariel give you?" A strange, sensual yearning filled Jackson's chest. He decided to kiss Alel's face off by the end of the night.

"I'm not going to tell you until after dinner, and then I'll show you." Alel rubbed behind his horn as he often did when he was nervous. It was too cute, and Jackson couldn't stand it. He grabbed the back of Alel's head and pulled him in for a kiss. The moan from Alel made Jackson break their kiss with a grin.

"You said cookies, right?"

"Yeah." Alel laughed. They ate in the kitchen, sandwiches, milk, and a platter of cookies. "I had chips, but Sariel ate them."

It was hard not to laugh at the thought of an angel baking cookies with a demon and stealing all his chips, but Jackson was glad he lived in such a world. He glanced at Alel, his smile growing wider.

"It's a little frightening how fond I am of you," Jackson confessed. "I've never had so much fun with a boyfriend before."

"I'm your boyfriend?" Alel's tail sped into double time as it wagged from side to side.

"We've been dating for almost a month." Jackson's face grew hot. "But if you don't want—"

Alel interrupted. "I do. I—"

Alel made a half-choked sound in the back of his throat. He jumped up from his chair and Jackson mimed him. For a moment he was worried, but Alel swept him up in a bear hug and nuzzled against his chest. Jackson kissed his horns while petting his hair.

"Hey, Alel?"

"Hmmm?"

"Weren't you going to show me something after dinner?"

"Yeah. It'll be more comfortable in the living room." They walked hand in hand to the sofa. Alel pointed to the rug. "Sit on the floor."

"Okay." Jackson bit his bottom lip. "I'm kinda nervous since I don't know what you're going to do, but I trust you, so..." He sat instead of finishing the sentence.

Meanwhile, Alel lit candles and turned on the radio. He smacked the lights off with his tail and sat on the sofa with his legs on either side of Jackson. Jackson held his breath when Alel touched his shoulders and then gave a loud, happy exhale when Alel began to knead into his muscles.

"This is nice—right there, Alel." Jackson shifted so Alel's thumb could hit a tight spot in Jackson's traps.

"Better?" Alel's voice was husky as he asked the question.

"Yeah, this is perfect. I didn't expect anything this nice."

"Good." Alel kissed the crown of Jackson's head.

His fingers spread out to the rest of Jackson's shoulders. His thumbs circled across Jackson's shoulder blades as his fingers kneaded the top of his back. Then he rolled his palms against Jackson's shirt.

"Want me to take off my shirt?" Jackson asked, irritated by the way the material bunched up around him.

"If you want," Alel said, his voice deeper and more velvety than earlier.

"It's not too much temptation, is it?" Jackson peeked over his shoulder. "You sound a little hot and bothered."

"It's because I'm thinking about touching your skin." Alel leaned close and kissed the shell of Jackson's ear, whispering in the same lush voice. "I promise to keep my hands well above your belt line. I'd chug a gallon of holy water before doing something I didn't think you'd want."

"I didn't want to make it harder on you than it already is." Jackson shrugged, guilty. "I know you're probably famished."

"Haven't you noticed there's no more circles under my eyes?" Alel's arms encircled him and his nose tickled the nape of Jackson's neck.

"Yeah, I thought you were extra tired when we first met?"

"I was low on energy."

"Because I can't feed you."

"But you *can*," Alel continued to whisper. "I realized it Wednesday when we were kissing."

Jackson shifted so he could glance over his shoulder. Alel kissed his temple.

"I can taste oranges, and fresh-baked blueberry muffins with real butter, and yogurt sweetened with honey."

"You...can *literally* taste muffins and yogurt? From a little backrub?"

"Yes."

"But I thought it had to be sex? Vampires have to drink blood."

"So did I, but I'm beginning to learn how everything I ever knew was a lie, and the only truth is..." he stopped.

"What were you going to say?" Jackson turned all the way around and looked up at Alel's eyes.

"The only truth I know is this—I want to see you every day, and I want to touch you." He brushed his hand up Jackson's cheek. "And when you die, I'll sneak into to heaven and steal kisses from your mouth, and if God forbids it, He'll have to destroy my soul because nothing short of oblivion will stop me."

"I can't breathe." Jackson pressed a hand to his chest. "That's...you're so...fuck, I can't talk, either." Jackson laughed. He was breathless and heady, but his entire mouth grinned, not just the corners, and his eyes glimmered with unspoken emotion.

Once he caught his breath, he slipped out of his shirt and let it fall onto the floor. He sat with his back to Alel again and flexed so Alel could stare at his back muscles. Alel gave a contented sigh as his hands settled back on Jackson's skin.

"Lie on your stomach."

Jackson obeyed, no longer hesitant. Alel straddled Jackson's ass and the shoulder rub turned into a full back massage. Jackson dissolved, all the tension leaving his body as Alel worked on his muscles.

"Your skin is soft," Alel whispered, kissing along Jackson's spine.

A moan escaped Jackson's mouth. The comforting weight of Alel's body, the pressure of his hands, the soft kisses dappling across Jackson's skin, all made him feel spectacular, as if he floated as Alel moved up and down his back with fingers and palms. Each kiss sent shivers up Jackson's spine.

Alel's kisses trailed across Jackson's shoulders. Jackson arched into them, enjoying them. He laughed, however, when Alel's erection kept poking at the cleft of his ass.

"Sorry." Alel pulled back and knelt beside Jackson.

"It's no problem." Jackson rolled into his side. Alel's face was flushed, his eyes dark and glittering, his lips plump and parted. Jackson's own cock was stiff—his body's reaction to Alel's hands and lips. "So...want to go make out on your bed for a while?"

Alel moaned and visibly shuddered at the mere suggestion. Jackson raced him to the bedroom. He left his shirt on the living room floor and pushed Alel onto the mattress. He lay on top on the incubus, pressed his tongue into his mouth, and then fumbled with the buttons on Alel's shirt. He opened the shirt, revealing Alel's bone-white chest, and flicked his tongue against Alel's lavender-colored nipple.

"Oh god! Oh god!" Alel wailed in pleasure, bucking his hips and puffing up his chest.

Jackson's flicking turned to sucking kisses. He rolled his tongue across the hard nub of one nipple and then bit his way over to the other one. Alel gripped the sheet. His tail whipped against them hard enough to tear the fabric, but he ignored the damage to his bedding. Jackson trailed additional kisses up and across Alel's collarbone, leaving hickies as placeholders to where he'd been. Jackson ended at Alel's mouth. He fisted both of Alel's horns and tugged them, bringing Alel's mouth closer for Jackson to claim.

"Are you horns longer?" Jackson asked as they paused to catch their breaths.

Alel nodded, red-faced and gasping and still gripping at the sheets. Curious, Jackson leaned up and kissed up each horn. His tongue reached out and he licked up the smooth surface of one, and then dropped lower and nibbled on Alel's elf-shaped ear.

"Oh fuck! I-I can't anymore!" Alel shoved Jackson to the side and scrambled off the bed. "I need a few minutes!"

Jackson lay on his back propped up on his elbows. The bathroom door banged shut and the sound of the shower water hissed through the hallway. He wondered if Alel was finishing himself off? Jackson bit the inside of his cheek, trying to figure out how he felt about the whole situation. Alel's massage was amazing. Other partners had offered, but it was always a sly attempt to get Jackson out of his pants, disguised as a romantic gesture, but not with Alel. Alel had meant the back rub as such. Jackson stood.

He didn't want Alel running off by himself for Jackson's sake, and he decided to check on him.

Chapter Six

HUMANS SANG *HOSANNA* as they stood in neat rows between pews. They shouted *hosanna* between the peals of church bells, but they did not know. *They did not know.* Alel's fingers gliding across the smooth, delicate skin of Jackson's back, *that* was joy. Alel's ragged breathing as Jackson consumed every inch of his torso with love bites, *that* was praise. Jackson's weight accidentally brushing against Alel's swollen cock as he shifted up to kiss his horns and then shimmied down to nibble on Alel's ear—*that was hosanna in the highest.*

And Alel wasn't strong enough for it. He swooped to the brink of climax and knew he'd tumble over the edge if he didn't put some physical distance between himself and Jackson.

In the bathroom, Alel tore off his pants and jumped into the shower. He turned the dial all the way to the right, as cold as he could get it. He'd always heard mention of cold showers shocking one out of arousal, but all the freezing jet managed to do was chill Alel's body and make him shiver, miserable from cold, and no less wanton for his suffering.

"Alel."

He jerked at the sound of Jackson's voice. He stared at the cream-colored tiles, too ashamed to meet Jackson's gaze. Alel shook and dripped icy water from his hair and the tips of his wings.

Jackson turned off the water and grabbed a towel. He pressed it against Alel's chest. Alel flinched at the pressure of it against his skin.

"I can't. I'm sorry. I'm trying. I'm trying so hard, but it was too good, and I was going to come and—"

"Shhhh, shhhh," Jackson stroked Alel's hair with one hand and dabbed the towel over his shoulders with the other.

His first hand dropped to Alel's cheek and he held it there as he graced Alel's mouth with several, calming kisses. Jackson pulled back, staring into Alel's eyes.

"I want you to feel good too." Jackson kissed each corner of his mouth. "Me not wanting to have sex doesn't mean you can't come at all. I'm sorry. I never meant to make you think you couldn't. I'm sorry."

"It doesn't gross you out?"

"What? No." Jackson showered Alel's face with quick pecks, each warm as a burst of light against Alel's skin. "I don't necessarily *dislike* the thought of sex. I'd rather kiss and cuddle instead, but—" Jackson brushed his nose against Alel's. "—I think watching you get excited enough to come might be fun."

"W-what if I get wound up and want to touch myself while we kiss? Would that be too much, or..." Alel's throat tightened, and he couldn't finish the question. He held his breath. His heart did flips in his chest at the thought of Jackson watching him.

"Why don't you finish drying off, and we'll go back to the bedroom and find out?" Jackson pinched Alel's nipple. Alel cried out and squirmed beneath Jackson's fingers. His stiff cock brushed against his own thigh, the cold useless in his attempt to calm it.

Alel ran the towel over his body, hissing as he dried his sensitive wings, tail, and erection. He slipped back into his boxer shorts, not wanting to be completely naked when Jackson wore pants, and walked back into the bedroom with the towel still in his hand. Nervous, his wings kept shifting and his tail curled and uncurled.

"I don't want you to tolerate this. I—I could wait until I'm alone." Alel sat on the bed, afraid to look at Jackson. "It won't be fun if you're not into it too."

"Let's try it." Jackson sat beside Alel, pulling one of his hands away from the towel so he could hold it. "No one's ever tried to compromise with me. It'll be fun to..." Jackson turned his head away, flustered. Alel glanced at him to make sure he was okay, but then Jackson's gaze returned to Alel with more confidence. "It'll be fun to experiment."

The intensity in his stare was all Alel needed to relax again. He tossed the towel to the floor and brushed his fingertips across Jackson's cheek. Jackson pulled Alel into his lap. He smoothed his thumbs across all the pretty bruises he'd marked onto Alel's skin, and Alel sighed and relaxed into the touch. Their lips drew near each other, hovering out of reach as their hands explored each other's bodies. Jackson took the lead, bridging the gap between them and sucking Alel's bottom lip. Alel shivered, not from cold but from anticipation. His fingers danced across Jackson's ribs as he prolonged touching himself until the last possible second when he couldn't stand it any longer.

Jackson gave no indication he was in a hurry. He dragged his lips up Alel's throat and slipped his right hand to the small of Alel's back in the sweet spot between his tail and wings which was still sensitive, but not so much that Alel couldn't control himself. Jackson's other hand wove into Alel's hair, tugging *just so* and making Alel moan into their kisses.

Alel's right hand rubbed up and down his alabaster leg, wanting to touch himself, but not quite confident enough. They continued to kiss...lips...throats...shoulders... They took their time. The only sign of impatience was in Alel's fingers, toying with his leg and the way his tail swished in overstimulated excitement.

Jackson's grip untangled from Alel's hair, and he laced his fingers with Alel's. They continued to kiss, holding hands and sliding their tongues together. Then Jackson guided Alel's hand to his own cock. He molded Alel's fingers around himself, a sculptor working clay into place. Alel gave an openmouthed cry midkiss. His cock was hard, hot, and throbbing in his own hand. He squeezed himself, and a jolt shot through him. Jackson sucked at his lips again, and Alel whimpered into each kiss as he palmed his own cock.

"Jackson." The name slipped from Alel's lips during an exhale. He trembled with each upstroke.

"You're beautiful," Jackson whispered against Alel's lips, pulling him in for another kiss.

Alel worked himself faster, struggling for each new breath until he couldn't kiss any longer. Alel curled against Jackson's shoulder while rocking his hips and jerking hard and quick at his own cock.

"Jackson, oh baby, oh baby, I'm going to come!"

Jackson kissed up the side of Alel's horn. They weren't as sensitive, but Jackson's lips against them as his orgasm swooped up from his belly was enough to catch the breath in Alel's throat as waves of hot semen splashed over his hand and thighs and stomach. It was unlike anything Alel had ever known. His usual orgasms were quick, sharp, trembling things, but as he sat in Jackson's lap—Jackson's lips on him and arms around him —the pleasure bloomed in Alel's center, ringing out as sweet as the last note in a song and lingering even after the music ended.

Then he was a ragdoll in Jackson's arms, grateful for the support. Jackson held him close, stroked his hair, and adorned his throat with soft, lazy kisses.

"I was right; that was fun to watch. Your reactions are...well, exciting."

"I've never felt this good in my life," Alel whispered as Jackson pulled both of them to the bed.

"Good." Jackson grinned and kissed Alel's lips.

"But, you really don't want to finish?" Alel studied Jackson's face.

"I-I don't know. Kinda, but...m-maybe after we date a little longer?" Jackson gave a nervous laugh. "If we're going to experiment, we can try different things as we go and decide what works, right?"

"Yeah, but you don't have to experiment." Alel shook his head.

"That's the thing." Jackson held Alel's face. "This is the first time I *could* explore what I want and don't want without someone pressuring me." He kissed Alel's forehead. "It's great."

"It's...the same for me." Alel smiled. "But with kissing and affection, instead of sex, so I guess it's actually the opposite side of it."

They kissed one last time and used the towel to wipe themselves down, and then snuggled beneath the duvet. They brushed their noses together, giving their lips a chance to rest from the searing friction of their earlier kisses.

"Don't leave." Alel wrapped his arms around Jackson. "Stay here and hold me until morning."

"I didn't bring a toothbrush."

"I don't care. I'll miss you if you leave."

"I'd miss you too." Jackson nuzzled against Alel's ear, kissing it. "I guess I could stay. I'll have to leave in the morning, though. I have a shoot tomorrow."

Alel nodded. He didn't want Jackson leaving in the morning either but understood. For the time being, he enjoyed having their arms locked together, Jackson's leg slung around him, and the shared warmth of their bodies beneath the covers.

"THIS IS A soap opera to you, isn't it?" Alel glared at the angel.

"Yes. There isn't much plot, but I'm enjoying the character development."

"Oh, go fuck yourself, Sariel."

"I wouldn't know how to." The angel looked smug as they sat on a park bench and parried words with Alel.

"I would imagine, for an angel, it'd involve a lot of stroking your own feathers and cursing under your breath." Alel returned the smug look, no longer flustered by the angel's teasing. Sariel was gorgeous as ever, but Alel had grown to appreciate their friendship, and Jackson filled up most of Alel's silk rope and rose petal fantasies these days (most of them).

"What are you thinking about?" Sariel asked. "You have a mischievous expression on your face."

"I was thinking about how cute you'd be if you were tied to my bed." Alel flicked his tail.

"You're so damn wicked." Sariel scowled. "Buy me popcorn to apologize."

"Can't apologize if I'm not sorry." Alel stood up and stretched. "But I supposed I should get you some popcorn for the trouble of dealing with me."

"Yes, you should." Sariel snorted, also standing.

They started walking down the streets in search of a store. The sparrows fought among maple branches from trees growing out of circles cut into the sidewalk. The sunlight angled off store windows, gilding the glass bright yellow-white.

"Caramel or cheddar?" Alel asked.

"I wouldn't even have a private spot," Sariel muttered, ignoring Alel.

"Somehow I don't think you're talking about popcorn?" Alel leaned against the bark of a maple and watched Sariel's confused, thoughtful expression.

"I mean, if I wanted to try, you know, and see how it felt. I'm an angel. We can't steal money or charm landlords into giving us free rent for a year. We don't need a place to live because we don't sleep, and we're supposed to spend all our time helping humans, but that means I don't have anywhere to go."

Alel laughed, hiding his face in his hand.

"What? I don't think this is funny at all. It's frustrating."

"Frustrated are you, little angel?"

"Shut up! It wasn't an innuendo." Sariel sulked, crossing their arms and glowing extra brightly. "But I am curious. We're not supposed to, but what if it's the same as demons and kissing?" Sariel frowned. "Maybe heaven also lies."

"Probably," Alel agreed. He took the spare key to his apartment off of his key ring and handed it to the angel. "Here, take this."

"Why?"

"I'm spending next weekend with Jackson."

"Did you want me to water your plants?"

"Holy fuck, Sariel. I'm giving you permission to borrow my apartment for a night."

"What? I couldn't! It seems rude? Somehow? It surely is rude."

"Yes, we wouldn't want to be rude to a demon—fucking take the key, Sariel. We're friends, right? It's no different than borrowing a cup of sugar from a neighbor, only significantly more hilarious."

"It'd be embarrassing," Sariel muttered, although they slipped the key into the pocket of their shift.

"I'm utterly useless as a demon now. The least you can do is help me create an angelic scandal so I can keep some of my pride."

"Stupid demon, pride is a sin."

"Thank God. I don't want to be too virtuous."

"You thanked the Lord." Sariel laughed.

"Fuck, I did." Alel sighed, but then he leaned forward with a sly grin. "Curse Him once for me this weekend, okay? Level out the playing field."

"I promise nothing." Sariel blushed. "But, thanks, for letting me borrow your place. I've never slept in a bed. It'll be nice."

"I'll be sure to stock the cupboards with chips. Now, did you want caramel or cheddar popcorn?"

IT'D BEEN THREE days of waiting and Sariel paced in front of the door, not quite daring to use the key clasped between their fingers.

"Okay, I've checked on all my humans. I swept the neighborhood and didn't see anyone needing guidance. It's only a quick pause from my duties." Sariel gave themself a nervous giggle. "Hell isn't going to open up and swallow me for taking a lunch break. Nothing bad happened to Alel when he broke taboo."

In fact, Alel looked marvelous. His skin glowed when he mentioned Jackson, his horns and hair gleamed darker than onyx, and he wasn't half as scrawny as he used to be. It was the happiest Sariel had ever seen Alel or Jackson in their entire lives, and Sariel was excited for both of them.

"Quit being afraid." Sariel squeezed the metal in their hand as they gave themself a lecture. "I'm an angel. We don't fear."

Sariel slipped the key inside the lock, fingers shaking too much to turn it. After a moment of fumbling, Sariel managed to open the door and ran inside. Sariel slammed the door, as if *that* would prevent anyone from seeing them enter. They rested a hand on their burning cheek and sucked in deep breaths to slow their shaky heartbeat.

Sariel tiptoed to Alel's bedroom. The angel knew no one was home, but couldn't help sneaking around instead of walking. They sat on the bed and noticed the blankets were freshly laundered, and the sheets were silk and cool against the angel's hand. A salt rock lamp sat on the nightstand. A soft, pinkish glow bathed the room in calming light.

"Stupid fucking demon," Sariel swore with affection and sighed. "I didn't ask you to make the room nice."

The angel loosened their shift and slipped it to their waist, tying it around them like a shenti. Sariel sat on the side of the bed. The bedroom was a gallery of paintings of lovely, naked forms, but to an angel, every creature was beautiful because they were the work of the Lord. Since nothing Sariel saw stirred the angel, Sariel closed their eyes.

Breathing slowly, Sariel reached up but hesitated and ended up brushing fingers against their arms instead. They kept their eyes closed and concentrated on the sensation of their touch against their own skin. Sariel relaxed after a moment and let their fingers explore higher up on their shoulders.

When the angel reached the soft feathers at the base of their wings, their breath hitched and they shuddered. Angels groomed each other, but only during special circumstances, and they weren't supposed to groom themselves, to avoid vanity, but it was elation and not vanity consuming Sariel. Sariel explored the softness of their own feathers and the warmth of the wing beneath them. A quiet sigh escaped Sariel's lips, and Sariel wrapped their wings around themself and lay on their side.

Sariel nuzzled against the side of their wing, moaning. Fluffy warmth surrounded them, and their fingers moved with clumsy, inexperienced strokes. The more Sariel fumbled their fingers through their feathers, the tighter their muscles contracted. Their petting grew quick and desperate.

Sariel spread their wings wide and raked their nails through their own plumage. They cried out and arched up, tugging at their feathers until the tight trembling somehow broke, and they moaned before crashing back onto the bed, dazed and panting and quite content.

Sariel wrapped themself in their wings again, but this time there was no urgency or need in the action, merely comfort. They grabbed half of the duvet and added it to the spiral of feathers and linen surrounding them.

Sleep came quickly and peacefully to Sariel as they lay rolled up in their wings and the scent of fabric softener from the duvet. Angels didn't sleep. They wandered and watched humans and helped when they could, although too often all they could do was pray and stay nearby to offer invisible comfort. However, Sariel decided naps were divine, and they would definitely take one again in the future.

A deep sleep enclosed around them. They didn't hear the front door rattle and click open, neither did they realize when another person walked into the bedroom until they started shaking Sariel.

"Get the fuck up, Alel. I haven't seen you in weeks. You know you get sick when you skip the clubs, so get up because we're going out tonight!"

Sariel's heart went mad in their chest, thrashing and beating against their ribcage. They didn't move, hoping whoever it was would go away.

"Alel!"

They pushed Sariel flat against the mattress, pulling back the comforter and jerking back when they saw a bright, golden angel, instead of the expected pale demon.

"Hello? And here I thought the idiot was starving himself again, but he's been feasting on you instead!"

"P-please don't tell anyone. I'll get into trouble," Sariel pleaded, still groggy from their first time sleeping and panicking because they'd been caught.

"It'll be our little secret." He stroked Sariel's cheek, licking his lips.

"Naberius, right?" Sariel asked.

They'd seen this incubus with Alel. Naberius in his natural form resembled a dragon more than a demon, tall and broad with mossy green wings and eyes and an olive tint to his complexion. Something about the way the demon's large, thick horns twisted up and out from above their temples looked attractive to the angel—which was odd because *attractive* wasn't typically a word Sariel used to describe anything.

"Yes," the incubus purred. "And what's your name, kitten?"

"Well, certainly not kitten." Waking up, Sariel realized Naberius still stroked their cheek, so they clasped the demon's hand and lowered it, *knowing* better than to let a demon touch them for too long. "It's Sariel."

"Lovely." Naberius leaned a little closer. "So, Sariel. Where's Alel?"

"Um, well, he's, uh, at the store, err, buying sex toys."

Self-gratifying wing play, slothfulness in sleep, lying—it was a good thing Sariel got on well with demons because they were rather sure they were going to end up in hell by the end of the night.

Naberius barked out in laughter. His voice dropped to a low, sultry tone once he calmed down. "And what sort of sex toys do angels use?"

"Oh, you know—the usual kinds."

"Be specific. I'm dying of curiosity." Naberius licked his lips again and squeezed Sariel's hand in his excitement.

"Well, let's see what I told him to buy..." Sariel's mind raced as they tried to remember what sort of sex toys he'd seen humans use. "A paddle, of course, and some taper candles, and fuzzy handcuffs, and lingerie, and strawberry-flavored gel that heats up and tingles when you blow on it." Sariel's imagination ran off on its own. It was always a little too fun to lie to demons. They believed anything Sariel said without question. "Of course, I was created after the Nephilim, so we can't do some things he'd want to do, but Alel's very creative—and wicked! He's the worst demon in all the bowels of hell. You should give him a promotion."

"Oh kitten, Alel is the *least* wicked demon I know. He's a lost puppy. Now if you wanted someone wicked—" Naberius leaned closer a second time. Their lips hovered a few inches apart. "I'd be happy to stay and show you what sort of pleasure a real incubus is capable of providing.

"I doubt you could." Sariel laughed, unable to censor themself.

"Want to bet?" Naberius pinned Sariel's hands over their head. He flexed his arms, showing off the thick knotted muscles in his biceps and chest.

"I'm too embarrassed! We don't even know each other!" Sariel screamed. A foreign, excited rush swooped through Sariel's belly, and suddenly, tingling strawberry goo and hot candle wax didn't seem half as funny as they seemed—God forgive Sariel—interesting.

"Don't be shy, kitten. We'll become good friends before the night's over."

"Um, you're, what I mean to say is it's a very nice offer, but I, uh... I'm nervous as it is, and I couldn't handle two demons at once. M-maybe after we get to know each other a little better?" Sariel's face burned. They averted their gaze away from Naberius's beautiful, spiraled horns. "Please go. I'm sorry, but please go."

"Kitten, I'm hurt!" Naberius pouted.

The wildest thought stole into Sariel's mind. Naberius's thick, calloused fingers searched through Sariel's feathers. The angel shuddered, all the tension from earlier returning, more needy and urgent than ever. The urge to struggle against Naberius—not to be let go, but rather to encourage the demon to grip more tightly—was so strong, new, desperate, and frightening that Sariel broke into tears.

"Wait, don't cry." Naberius released Sariel's wrists and sat them upright while holding their shoulders. "Don't cry. I'll go. Don't cry. Your coating my tongue in salt. I didn't mean to ruin the mood."

"This is all so confusing!" Sariel curled against Naberius's chest and clung to his shirt with both hands. "I shouldn't want any of this, but I do."

"It's fine. It's fine. Your side is forgiving, so don't feel bad." Naberius patted Sariel's back, trying to comfort the angel, but his hand landed right between Sariel's wings and the gentle touch sent jolts throughout Sariel's body.

"Goddamn!" Sariel screamed with a raw, shaking voice. Sariel pressed hard against Naberius's chest, grabbed him by the horns, and pulled them together until their teeth clacked in a rough, graceless kiss. Sariel hoped the kiss would spur the demon on, make him push Sariel back against the mattress, but Naberius whimpered and then jerked away.

"You-you—holy fucking goddamn."

"I-I'm sorry. I forgot demons don't kiss."

"I have to go." Naberius jumped to his feet. "Tell Alel I'll catch him later." Naberius fled from the apartment.

Chapter Seven

"HOW'D I LET you talk me into this!" Alel laughed, holding onto a nearby rail to keep himself standing as he tried to balance himself on a pair of rollerblades.

"Come on. It's easy. Here, hold my hands, and I'll help."

Alel reached for Jackson's hands but ended up wrapping his arms around his shoulders so he could stay upright.

"You need to relax, or you'll keep falling."

"I'm not meant for this."

"Everyone starts by falling." Jackson snuck a kiss onto Alel's cheek as they clung together. "Try again."

Alel's breath caught. He glanced around, always checking for nearby demons, always paranoid he'd get caught on a date and dragged away, but no one ever saw them. Alel stood up, wobbling on his skates. After several tries, he managed to stand with only one hand bracing against Jackson.

"Okay, let's go slow," Jackson urged.

They managed several strides before Alel toppled onto the concrete. He rubbed above his tail, groaning in pain from how he landed.

"It's almost as bad as getting kicked in the nuts."

"You want to quit?"

"No." Alel clambered back up. He shot Jackson a flirtatious glare. "The things I do for you."

Jackson kissed the tip of Alel's nose in appreciation, making Alel blush fiercely. After thirty more minutes of Alel falling on his ass, they unlaced the skates and carried them back to a blanket they had spread out near the duck pond. They took turns reaching into a bag of pellets and tossing them into the water for the ducks to bicker over.

"So how was your shoot yesterday?"

"Great. The model was a gorgeous werewolf and she had the longest, thickest hair I've ever seen."

"How do you know she was a werewolf?"

"The eyes. The camera sees everything. She mentioned she'd been vegan for over ten years, and the makeup and hair crew were teasing her about it, but *I'm* freaking glad she doesn't eat people. It can't be easy to go against your nature, so if she wants to brag about it a little, let her. I shared my favorite vegan blogs with her."

"I wonder how much shit she gets from her pack?"

"She doesn't have one."

"Did she say that to you?"

"No, but the camera also picks up on loneliness."

"I know how she feels." Alel snorted while tossing another fistful of pellets into the water. "I'm not lonely anymore, though."

Jackson's fingers laced with his, and he smiled. They lay back with their fingers still interlocked and gazed up at the clouds.

"Alel."

"Hmmm?" Alel hummed, and he gave their perimeter another once-over.

"I love you."

Alel forgot about the possibility of other demons. He turned onto his side and stared at Jackson, who turned his head and smiled back at Alel. Alel rolled on top of Jackson, dropping his glamour for a moment, drawing Jackson's bottom lip with the tips of his fingers.

"I think I love you too. They say demons can't love, but I don't know how else to describe how I feel about you."

They tangled their arms around each other, bumping their noses and teasing one another by not quite kissing until both their hearts protested, and they forfeited to the natural pull of their mouths. They indulged in languid kissing for as long as they dared. Alel pulled back and slipped his glamour on before someone screamed.

"Yes, I definitely love you."

"I definitely love you too." Jackson squeezed Alel in his arms.

"Make pizza tonight?"

"I'll add garlic this time." Jackson laughed.

They dumped the last few pellets into the pond, folded their blanket, and held hands as they walked to the store. After dinner, they turned on the TV and crowded together on the couch. Alel sat in Jackson's lap, brushing the tip of his nose along Jackson's neck, and kissing Jackson's skin at random intervals. Jackson turned to Alel. His eyes shimmered in the TV light.

"Hey, Alel?"

"Yeah?"

"I want to take some pictures of you. Would you mind?"

"I don't mind."

"Naked."

"I don't think I heard—"

"I want to do a full shoot of you naked. I want to see you through the lens. I want to see the real you."

Alel's face turned an instant and beautiful shade of peony. He nodded and Jackson stole a quick kiss.

"Let me grab my camera and set up the bedroom so we can get started."

ALEL STARED AT how Jackson had converted his bedroom into a mini studio. White sheets draped against the walls and the shades were all removed from the room's lamps to provide better lighting.

"Ready?" Jackson asked while fidgeting with his camera.

Alel struggled out of his shirt, careful to keep his wings from snagging the fabric. Slipping his tail out of his pants was easier, and once naked, Alel caught his reflection in the full-length mirror hanging on Jackson's closet door.

His hair had grown past his shoulders in the last month, so he kept it pulled back. His horns now the curling spirals of a ram's, and Alel realized he had the sort of cliché, heart-shaped mouth he always admired on women. He would never be as buff as Naberius. However, Alel's slender body now had the suggestion of muscle beneath the milky-white skin. It wasn't the body of a weightlifter, but perhaps a yoga instructor, lithe and subtle in its strength.

"I don't even recognize myself," he said.

"I'm glad you kept the freckles. I'd be sad if they somehow disappeared." Jackson walked over to Alel, lavishing kisses on the purple flecks adorning Alel's pale skin. He grinned and brushed his hand against Alel's warm cheek. "The blush will be a nice touch to the photographs."

"Do you want me to stand in front of the bed, or..."

"I want you on the bed." Jackson wore the grin of a Cheshire cat and something about the expression rushed blood straight to Alel's cock. He knelt on the bed and continued to watch Jackson as he glanced through the lens.

"Okay. Ready?" He asked.

Alel nodded.

Jackson snapped a few pics without ceremony. Alel stuck his tongue out and laughed as his tail flicked merrily behind him. He opened his mouth to ask if they were almost done, but Jackson spoke first.

"Okay, good. Nice warm-up shots. Now touch yourself."

"What?" Alel was sure he misunderstood the order.

Jackson peeked from behind the camera, mouth still curved into a trickster-cat's smile. "You heard me. Touch yourself."

"How's this?" Alel grabbed his left shoulder and rested his other hand on his thigh.

"Beautiful. Now grab your cock."

Alel swallowed and stared at Jackson behind his camera. The air was savory as *bouchée à la reine,* prepared by scratch in a farmhouse kitchen in the French countryside. Alel braced one hand against the mattress, so Jackson's camera had a good angle of his body as he grabbed his shaft and thumbed the slit at his cockhead.

Alel panted as tremors shivered through him. He smeared precome across his head and slammed his fist to his base, pulling to the top. Alel's moans poured free and loud. Jackson watching him made Alel feel like a dozen attentive hands caressed him, and it was an exquisite meal, hearty and rich and decadent.

"Good. Good," Jackson cooed, camera clicking with each shot. "Use your tail now."

Alel spiraled his tail around his own cock, wrapping his fingers on top of it and double stroking himself.

"Spread out your wings," Jackson ordered.

Alel reached them out as far as he could. His mouth hung open so he could both gasp for air and call out in ecstasy.

"Keep using your tail and touch your wings." Jackson's own voice sounded excited as he watched.

Alel closed his left wing and folded it across his chest to make it easier to run his fingers up and down the smooth scales of his outer wing. Alel wanted to go slowly. He wanted to tease the camera, but he only managed three long glides of his fingers. Alel gasped, shook, and rubbed wide circles against his scales before pouring out over his tail and belly. He curled into a ball and gasped for breath. His heartbeat blasted like the trumpets calling forth the End of Everything.

"Lick your tail clean."

"Fuck, Jackson." The words came out as a wheeze as Alel struggled to catch his breath.

Alel looked up, but Jackson was hiding behind the camera. Nevertheless, Jackson's excitement radiated through the air, making Alel tremble. He lifted his tail to his mouth, stretched out his tongue, and scooped the tip of his tongue up the smooth skin, catching every drop of come.

"I could make a fortune off these pictures." Jackson never stopped photographing as Alel continued to lick himself clean. "But these are staying in my private collection because I'd rather keep you all to myself."

"Greedy," Alel teased, his voice a tremulous, aroused whisper.

"You're still hard."

"Because you don't want to stop yet," Alel explained. "I could go all night if you wanted me to."

"I'll get a towel to clean your stomach."

Jackson rested his camera on its tripod and rushed out of the room, returning with a wet and a dry washcloth. He claimed several kisses for himself, before wiping up Alel's stomach and thighs. Once Alel sat clean and dried, Jackson returned to his place behind the lens.

"Can you get on all fours and stroke yourself?"

Alel stared right at Jackson, ignoring the camera. His tail rose in the air, an exclamation point announcing his excitement. He bit his bottom lip, stroking until his cock burned with fervent, unresolved tension.

"Alel, you're so hot." Jackson sighed, his camera never slowing its shooting. "When we're done shooting, I'm going to lick your neck and kiss you until you moan."

Alel moaned at Jackson's words. He reached around with his free hand and stuffed two fingers up his ass, needing the experience of being filled. Alel imagined Jackson behind him, ramming his hard cock over and over into Alel's tight ass until they both came with each other's names springing from their throats.

"Jackson!" He wailed as three distinct waves of come splashed onto Jackson's bed sheets. Alel didn't mind the mess. He dropped onto his belly and trembled as pleasant aftershocks teased his nervous system.

"Holy shit, Alel," Jackson whispered. His camera lay forgotten in his hands as he stared at Alel directly.

"I was thinking about you and got too excited," Alel confessed. "Maybe I shouldn't have? I probably shouldn't think about us having sex."

Jackson placed the camera in its tripod and raced to the bed. He shoved Alel onto his back and ran his tongue across Alel's lips. Alel opened his mouth and twisted their tongues together. The kisses were hungry and wet. Alel slipped his fingers beneath Jackson's shirt so he could feel out the ridge of Jackson's spine and knead loving, careful circles into Jackson's back muscles. Jackson kissed Alel's mouth raw and dropped beside him panting. A spark of desire shimmered from Jackson's body like a mirage, wavy, faint, unsolid.

"You should let me take your picture," Alel said after considering what his next move should be.

He didn't think Jackson wanted sex, but he seemed to want something. Their kisses had been bold and relentless, and yet their caresses had been loving, none of the urgent fumbling that led to undressing and petting. Still, there was a spark of want radiating from Jackson's spirit.

"No way are you touching my equipment."

Alel snorted. He reached into Jackson's pocket and stole his cell phone, activating the camera and snapping a picture of them side by side on the mattress.

"I'll text it to you," Jackson said.

"Do you want to..." He let the sentence hang.

Jackson bit his bottom lip, thinking.

"I don't know."

"I didn't mean sex, but I thought maybe—"

Jackson silenced him with a kiss, grinning. "I know what you meant. It's okay. I'm...unsure myself. I've never let anyone watch me and it...it'd be big, you know?" Jackson toyed with Alel's hair. "You said you were thinking about us?"

"Sorry—"

"Shhhh." Jackson kissed him. "I do, too, sometimes. Usually it's kissing...but not always, so don't worry."

"Oh." Alel's heart sped up. "Good, because I love thinking about you." Alel blushed. "I think about kissing more than you might think. I'm a terrible demon."

"But you're a terrific boyfriend." Jackson winked. "What if I turned off the lights? And kept the blanket over me?"

"Can I, um, at the same time on my own side of the bed?"

"I think I'd prefer it more if you did it at the same time." Jackson's eyes gleamed.

"Get comfortable." Alel scrambled to his feet to hit the lights and turn off the extra lamps as Jackson snuggled beneath the covers.

Alel lay with the blanket over him. He decided to start right away, so he grabbed his cock and eased his fist up and down. He heard a slight hitch of breath beside him. The mattress shook as Jackson also stroked himself. Alel closed his eyes and enjoyed both his own pleasure and little hints of Jackson doing the same. A tiny groan broke through the dark from Jackson's side of the mattress. The bed trembled a little faster.

"Oh God," Alel sighed. "It's so nice, knowing you're beside me."

"It's—not—frustrating?" Jackson asked, clearly short of breath as he grew closer to his climax.

"Why would—it be?" Alel asked in return, also winded.

"Because it's not—more?"

"It's—*ahh*—*it's*—Jackson—can we hold hands?"

"You—you—want to—hold hands? Don't you want—"

"I want to touch you. I don't care how."

Jackson's hand bumped against his beneath the covers. Alel laced their fingers together and squeezed. Alel moved his fist as fast as possible, his other hand locked with Jackson's. His chest felt bright inside, his cheeks burned like hellfire. He imagined a current of energy flowing between their clasped hands, making his body tingle as his cock throbbed.

"Alel! I'm close!"

"Yes! So-am-ahhh! Ahhh!"

"Oh, oh, Alel, oh!"

Jackson's grip tightened and the mattress's shaking reached a crescendo. Alel held his breath and came for a third time; only this time a thick wave of satisfaction washed over him because of Jackson finishing at the same time. Alel groaned, sinking heavily into the mattress as the tension drained from his muscles.

"Oh...that was nicer than I thought it'd be. I wouldn't mind doing it again," Jackson whispered, his thumbnail grazing along Alel's wrist. "It was even better while holding your hand. We were together even though we weren't, well, *together*."

Alel pulled Jackson into his chest, draping his tail over Jackson's hip. Jackson gave a nervous giggle, reaching out and running his fingers lightly across the length of Alel's tail.

"How does it feel?" Jackson asked.

"Like this." Alel thumbed Jackson's nipple through the cotton of his T-shirt. "Near the base, it'd feel more sensual, but the tip's less sensitive—which is good because I tend to smack it against things." Alel gave a small chuckle and wrapped his arm back around Jackson.

"If I'm getting you too worked up, let me know."

"I'm relaxed right now." Alel kissed Jackson's shoulder. "It feels nice, but I'll let you know if I start to get too bothered."

They lay together for several minutes, Jackson giving Alel's tail light brushes with his fingers while kissing his horns. When his touches started to warm Alel below the belly, he took Jackson's hand and kissed it to let Jackson know he should stop. Alel buried himself in Jackson's chest, sucking in Jackson's scent through his clothes.

"I love you," Alel muttered into Jackson's shirt, and the words earned him kisses across his brow and cheeks.

HE DIDN'T EXPECT Sariel to be there when he got home, but neither did he expect half a dozen angel feathers dotting the folds of an unmade bed. The white plumes glittered like fresh snow in the morning sunlight. Alel picked one up and stared at it for a full minute before letting it drop from his hand. The feather seesawed to the periwinkle-colored silk sheets Alel had put out solely for his friend's benefit, figuring the silk would feel luxurious against his feathers.

Alel turned and grabbed a hoodie. He marched through the streets in search of the angel. He searched until sunset and cursed heaven for not allowing angels to carry cell phones. He stopped at a store and bought a bought a bag of barbeque chips and a prepaid phone. Alel walked through the streets with the gifts as if he could lure the angel out of hiding in the same way one might use a can of tuna to call a cat home, but no angel came scurrying from the bushes to greet Alel as he meandered back toward his apartment.

He'd never needed the angel before. Sariel had a way of appearing whenever Alel stood alone or sat on park benches or at bus stops while watching the sun rise. When he reached his apartment, Alel tossed the chips and phone onto the couch and dropped to his knees, clasping his hands together.

"You said you'd be my guardian angel, so I'm praying for you to get your ass over here right now!" He thought the pounding on the door was an answer to his prayer, so Alel scrambled to his feet and threw the door open.

"There you are, you bastard!" Naberius slung both his arms around Alel's neck, relying on Alel for support. "You've been holding out on me. S'mean. I share, don't I?"

"Naberius, you're smashed out of your skull? What's wrong with you?" Alel dragged him into the living room, shut the door, and cursed his luck.

"Ate too much." Naberius groaned, hiding his face against Alel's shoulder. "Puked. Felt bad. Got drunk. It's your fault."

"My fault?"

"Yeah, look at you." Naberius dragged a heavy palm down Alel's cheek. "You're gorgeous now, so damn gorgeous. Bet you're sweeter than ice cream. Lemme have a lick."

Naberius leaned forward. Alel backed away when their lips almost brushed together.

"What does that have to do with you being drunk?"

"*The angel*," Naberius hissed.

"What did you do to Sariel?" Alel clenched Naberius's collar and slammed him against the wall, shaking the pictures in their frames beside them from the impact.

"Fuck you! *She* took advantage of *me*!"

"Ha! An angel taking advantage of a demon, that's rich. Exactly how does that work?"

Naberius's expression grew horror-stricken. He reached up, pinching his bottom lip and staring toward the bedroom. Alel's mouth dropped.

"Naberius, I need you to tell me what happened. The angel wasn't here when I came home, and I'm worried."

"Worried." Naberius snorted drunken, whiskey-scented laughter onto Alel's face.

"Sariel is my friend."

"You mean your lover. Do you subjugate yourself to that sort of filth to get a quick meal out of an angel?"

"I'm not justifying anything to *you*. Now what the fuck happened last night?"

"Th' dirty bitch kissed me! All I was trying to do was be friendly and fuck her. She had no right to kiss me!"

"Then what happened?"

"I ran away! I wasn't about to stick around for any more of that sick shit!" Naberius played with his lips again. He gave Alel a pitiful look and held onto Alel's shoulders. "I don't feel well. I'm gonna—I'm gonna be sick again."

"God dammit." Alel half dragged Naberius to the bathroom and got him on his knees in front of the toilet in time for the show.

The bathroom light painted everything in harsh tones, and the green of Naberius's wings was a jarring contrast to the white-tiled floor. Mad as he was, Alel couldn't help patting Naberius's hair as he purged the liquor from his guts. Alel knew, from experience, Sariel's misguided affection was terrifying, although he also wondered what made Sariel go for a kiss instead of a hug with Naberius. He fetched a glass of water and gave it to Naberius who washed his mouth out in the sink. Afterward, they stumbled to the bedroom and crashed onto the bed.

"Lie down. Relax. You're okay." Alel stroked his hair with each statement and fluffed the pillows beneath his head.

"Her feathers are still in the bed."

Naberius plucked a glittering feather from the sheets and twirled it in his fingers. Naberius closed his eyes, brushing the feather tip against his lips and shuddering. Alel watched, baffled and amused in equal measures.

"How do you seduce an angel, anyway?" Naberius asked, still toying with Sariel's feather.

"You hold hands and you talk a lot. Sariel loves salty food, so French fries, fried pickles, pretzels, chips; offer them something to nibble on and they'll talk to you—that's not a euphemism. I mean offer a real snack. Naberius, angels aren't humans. You can't shove it in and then go to sleep."

"But...she's food. You were using her to get healthy—angel food cake." Naberius laughed at his own lame joke.

"Sariel is not food. Sariel is my friend. Sariel is also an angel created after the flood and, therefore, not a she. You should probably know that if you want to court them."

"Who said anything about courting?" Naberius wrinkled his brow. He moved the feather down to his chest and held it there while frowning at Alel. "You know it's dangerous to make it sound like...like it's more than taking energy."

"It is more."

"Bullshit. She—the angel—told me about you two."

"You should also know Sariel is a liar, so whatever Sariel told you last night was probably a lie."

"You're a fucking liar too."

"True." Alel smiled, sitting up.

"Don't go." Naberius clung to the hem of Alel's shirt.

"I know you're sick, so stay here and sober up. If Sariel comes back, there's a bag of chips on the couch and a cell phone. Teach them how to use it for me."

"Where are you going?"

"To search the city. I'm sure Sariel is as freaked out as you right now. I need to find the little brat."

"I don't want to be alone." Naberius clung to Alel's shirt. He buried his face against Alel's body. "Stay here. Fuck me and make me better. Please. Please, you know I've never begged in my life, but I want you to take me right now, Alel. Make me forget about kissing, or fucking kiss me yourself if you're into it, just...please."

"You asshole." A melancholy laugh escaped him, as he ignored the strawberry-daiquiri flavor of Naberius's desire. "All those nights in bed together and never once did you let me fuck you. All those times could have been beautiful, and you were always too busy stuffing your face, and *now, now* you want me. Why? Because I'm pretty?" Alel stood up.

"Because I don't feel good," Naberius whined. "And because I'm scared! I want to feel better."

"I know kisses are frightening." Alel sighed. "But nothing's wrong with you except you're drunk. Sleep it off. I won't keep you alone any longer than I have to, but right now, I have to make sure Sariel isn't handling this as badly as you are—and they probably are."

"You both better come back, and we better fuck until dawn."

"You're so dumb." Alel couldn't keep the affection out of his voice. He kissed the crown of Naberius's head.

"Nasty," Naberius muttered and rubbed his head.

"I know all those times you dragged me into bedrooms with you was your way of taking care of me," Alel said.

"Shut up. It's not safe."

"Naberius, you don't have to watch over me anymore. I'm okay now." Alel stooped to give Naberius's forehead another kiss.

"I know, stupid. I knew the second I saw you. Look at you, a real fucking incubus now."

"We can feed off kisses," Alel whispered. "I fell in love with a human."

"You're lying."

"Or maybe you're so drunk none of this is real." Alel faked a laugh.

"Alel, god dammit, you better be lying."

"I need to find Sariel. I'll check on you as soon as I know they're safe."

"Whatever. I don't wanna deal with this." Naberius's eyes closed, his expression peaceful as he clutched Sariel's feather to his chest.

"Kissing's still gross," he muttered.

"Yeah? Then I'll stop kissing your forehead."

"I never said stop," Naberius growled. "Just that you're a freak. I should have known. You always called the main courses by name."

"Sleep here, okay?" Alel teased Naberius with another forehead kiss. "Don't wander off until you're sober."

Naberius sighed, already falling into a drunken sleep. Alel pried his shirt away from Naberius's fingers and used the opportunity to sneak out of the apartment. He alternated between walking and jogging until he stood in front of Jackson's door. Jackson answered wearing pajamas and looking more adorable than he had a right to. Alel stopped and stared.

"Alel?"

"Sorry, I know you work in the morning." Alel shook his head to clear it.

"Missed me?" Jackson stepped aside to let Alel in and gave him a welcoming kiss.

"Always," Alel sighed into the kiss. "But I'm here to ask a weird favor."

"What?"

"Um, don't suppose you could pray for guidance for me?"

"What's the matter? Can't demons pray?" Jackson chuckled.

"Sariel's avoiding me, but they can't ignore a human."

"You're using me to collect call an angel?" Jackson crossed his arms over his chest, visibly annoyed.

"I'm worried. Something happened between Sariel and Naberius, and now I have a drunk demon in my bed, demanding I fuck him, and an angel who's MIA."

"Okay...I'm intrigued enough to forgive you, but I doubt *me* praying is going to help." Jackson closed his eyes, head bowed and hands clasped.

"Dammit, Alel, god dammit." Sariel's sobs echoed from the kitchen.

"Are you okay?" Alel dragged Sariel to the sofa as Jackson stared in amazement.

"I fucked up so bad." Sariel smeared tears on the sleeve of their robe. "Naberius broke in and surprised me while I was sleeping. I didn't want us to get into trouble, so I lied and pretended we were lovers, but I got flustered and started crying, and Naberius tried to comfort me and patted my back, and everything *rushed* after that. The touch brushed my wings. It was incredible! So I grabbed him and kissed him, and then he ran away—"

"Sariel. Breathe."

"I feel horrible. He must be scared and confused right now, and it's all my fault."

"Are *you* okay?" Alel asked.

"I'm the worst angel ever." Sariel buried his face against Alel's chest.

"Hey." Jackson rested a hand on Sariel's shoulder, careful to avoid his wing. "Would you like a cup of tea?"

"I've never drunk tea." Sariel sniffed. "I could give it a try."

"I'll brew a cup for you." By the time Jackson returned with three cups of chamomile tea, the angel's tears were only stains on their blotchy cheeks.

"I'm sorry," Sariel said as they took the first teacup. "You deserve a better guardian angel than me."

"You're the one who told Alel to go to the party where he met me, right?"

"Yeah." A weak smile fought for a place on Sariel's lips. "I knew his glamour wouldn't work on you, and I was hoping you'd both get along."

"We do, and I think you're a better angel than you give yourself credit for."

"Are you going to be okay?" Alel asked.

"Yeah." Sariel nodded. "Thanks for worrying about me, but I'm okay Although I feel wretched for what I did to Naberius."

"About him—I better go home and check on him. He drank himself sick."

"I can go with you." Sariel set their empty cup on the coffee table. "The least I can do is apologize."

"Now's not a good time." Alel rubbed the bridge of his nose. "He's worked up and needy right now. You wouldn't last five seconds with him without getting pawed at, groped, and otherwise fondled. It's better I deal with him."

"I doubt he'd want to touch me after the other night," Sariel traced patterns against the lap of their robe.

"When I left he was holding one of your feathers to his chest."

"He was?" Sariel flushed.

"After brushing it against his lips."

"I-I should definitely apologize," Sariel muttered, refusing to meet either Alel's or Jackson's gazes. "Maybe explain the truth to him."

"Oh, so you actually know how to tell the truth?" Alel teased.

The tang of *saladitos* and *pulparindo* coated Alel's tongue. The angel's lust reminded Alel of the time Naberius dragged Alel to Mexico for tequila and one-night stands. The entire trip Naberius had eaten lollipops of dried mango rolled in chili powder and lemon-flavored *saladitos*, and

Alel had stuck to *señoritas* because he preferred the saffron rice of one-night stands to the actual candy sold at every store they visited.

Alel wrinkled his face at the odd mix of sweet, salty, citrus, and spicy, and missed the fresh-baked bread taste he had grown to associate with their friendship. Now he understood why Sariel hugged him and kissed Naberius, and for the first time, Alel thought of *compatibility* and not only sex.

"Do you want to go?" Alel held both of Sariel's shoulders, studying them to make sure the angel wasn't wanting something they'd regret later.

"I do," Sariel whispered, and the flavor of strange candy became unbearable in Alel's mouth.

"You still have my key, right?"

"Yeah?"

Alel glanced at Jackson. "Could I crash on your couch tonight?"

"Yeah?" Jackson echoed Sariel's confused tone. Alel reminded himself neither one of them could *taste* the tension in the air. Alel smirked

"Since you still have a key, you should check on Naberius while I stay here."

"You want me to go...alone?" Sariel asked.

"Only if you want to," Alel said.

"I...guess I could?" Sariel gave Alel another confused look. "Don't you want to sleep in your own bed?"

"You understand, right? Naberius is in a mood. He doesn't want a friend tonight. Do you still want to go?"

"Yes."

"There's a bag of chips for you on the sofa and a cell phone—I don't want to have to scour the city for you next time." Alel ruffled the angel's gold hair.

"I'm not supposed to own anything material, Alel."

"And I'm not supposed to spend an entire day searching for a bothersome angel because I'm worried about them. Life is difficult, isn't it?"

"Okay." Sariel sighed, toying with their fingers. "I'll keep the phone, but if I get sent to hell because you're a bad influence on me, I will not rest until you're sainted by the pope."

"Good luck on that." Jackson laughed as he gathered up their teacups.

"So," Sariel bit his bottom lip, staring at Alel for a moment longer. "I guess I should go and make sure he hasn't trashed your apartment, right?"

"He's sleeping like a baby."

Sariel managed a rather wicked grin for an angel. "Well then. He woke me up last time. It's only fair I do the same."

Chapter Eight

IT WAS SURREAL to watch the angel, who had appeared in Jackson's kitchen from nowhere, leave out the front door. "What did you do? You remind me of a cat who's dropped a dead snake in someone's shoe and you can't wait until they find the surprise." Jackson noted the dumb grin on Alel's face and the way his tail waved back and forth.

"I only did what Sariel did to me—set up a situation—and now I'll have to wait to see what happens, but I'm pretty sure I already know."

"The other incubus isn't going to hurt or molest Sariel, is he? Because if someone messed with my guardian angel, I'd punch their face flat—demon or not."

Alel wiped his mouth and then licked his lips to re-wet them. Jackson could tell he was thinking, by the crease in his brow.

"The only flavors I've ever been able to coax out of Sariel are a few snacks and fresh bread. I think it's because we're friends? Which, the thought of getting any sort of energy out of a friendship is absolutely insane, so much so I used to confuse it with physical desire, but when I spoke with Sariel, I tasted Naberius's favorite candy. I'm not sure if it makes sense if you can't taste it yourself, but Sariel knows exactly what they're in for at my place."

"So that's why you're wearing a shit-eating grin. You're getting back at Sariel for hooking us up."

"It is a nice bonus." Alel shrugged, his tail still waiving. "I feel empathetic toward Naberius. He got his first dose of affection, and it confused him so badly he went out and made himself sick, but Sariel will be good for him. It's about time that fat bastard eats some real food instead of pigging out on junk every night."

"It doesn't bother you?" Jackson asked, biting his lower lip. "Being stuck on the sofa while they fool around?"

"I hate *pulparindo*." Alel stuck out his tongue while wrinkling his face.

"What?"

"Mexican candy. I think it's gross. Sariel's desire is salty and lemon-flavored. It was making me queasy."

"But weren't you and Naberius—"

"Yeah, we were." Alel sighed.

"And you're not jealous of Sariel?"

"No. Besides, see my ribs?" Alel pulled up his shirt, exposing the contours of his body.

"Not half as much as I used to."

"Exactly."

"Hey, Alel?"

"Hmm?"

"How do I taste?" Jackson stepped closer, not sure how much proximity had to do with Alel's ability to feed.

Alel held Jackson's face with both hands. He brushed their noses together and nuzzled against the side of Jackson's neck.

"You're different every time. Right now, you're pho with fresh Thai basil and chili oil." Alel ghosted his lips up Jackson's throat. He brought their lips slightly out of reach from each other and blushed before dropping his hands and turning away. "Um, could you make up the couch for me?"

But the tender way in which Alel had held Jackson's face and the soft brushes of his nose and lips against Jackson's skin had left Jackson wanting more. He cupped Alel's cheek.

"I wouldn't mind cuddling if you wanted to sleep with me tonight."

Jackson loved the way Alel's eyes dilated whenever he suggested any small thing to Alel, as if Jackson was offering the incubus three wishes instead of some snuggle time.

"I'd love to." He stepped back, breaking Jackson's hold on him. "But between Naberius pawing over me while drunk, and Sariel yearning for him, I'm sort of worked up." Alel's face dropped into a miserable expression. "I can't help reacting to their energy."

"It's all right." Jackson grabbed Alel's hand and pulled him toward the bedroom. "We can calm you down a little before going to sleep."

He lay Alel against the comforter and settled on top of him. Alel's chest rose and fell as he panted through parted lips. A sharp sting of pain bit into Jackson's calf.

"Ow." Jackson jerked his leg and glanced behind him. "Your tail finally got me. I was wondering when it'd happen."

"I'm sorry." Alel tried to squirm out from under Jackson, but Jackson pinned him in place, so he said, "Maybe I should sleep on the sofa after all."

"But I have you right where I want you." Jackson kissed the tip of Alel's nose. "Stay put."

Jackson crawled off the bed and rushed to the kitchen. He rummaged through his liquor cabinet until he found a bottle of Crown Royal tucked away in a purple drawstring bag. He ditched the bottle and brought the bag with him to the bedroom.

"Would this be offensive?" Jackson asked, unsure of incubus culture short of "if it's nice, Alel probably wasn't allowed to do it."

"Makes me think of an incubus condom." Alel's lips twitched up in a half grin. He stretched out his tail so Jackson could cover the sharp barb with the bag.

"How does this feel?" Jackson slipped the bag over Alel's barbed tip and pulled the strings so it held in place.

"Heavy." Alel flicked his tail. "Not uncomfortable, though. I don't mind. Now I don't have to worry about hurting you when you're close." After the word close, Alel lidded his eyes, beckoning Jackson to get back into bed.

He returned to his spot on top of Alel, his hands toying with Alel's chest. They wandered to his corn silk textured hair.

"I love your purple freckles." Jackson bent and smothered Alel's face with kisses, catching all the areas of his nose and cheeks dotted with flecks of lavender.

"At least the rest of me is attractive now."

"I always thought you were attractive." Jackson frowned at the comment. "Your glamour was boring."

"I looked awful without it—"

"You looked sick. Now you look healthy." A soft smile washed over Jackson's face as he leaned close and pressed his forehead against Alel's. "I'm so happy. I was afraid dating me would hurt you, but you got healthier, instead. And you're always so considerate, even tonight you offered to sleep on the couch." Jackson opened his eyes, locking his gaze with Alel's. "I love you so much."

Alel flushed, his eyes bright and glassy. His tail whacked against Jackson's calf, but the velvet bag buffered the impact. Joy fizzed up in Jackson's chest He loved how Alel's tail gave his emotions away even when he was too flustered to say anything out loud.

"How do I taste?" Jackson asked. Alel explained his emotions better in food terms.

Alel closed his eyes, licking his lips. "Right now, champagne and blueberry stilton. When we start kissing the flavors will change, maybe roasted duck and chutney? I can tell you're happy because the food is rich."

"Yeah, I'm really happy right now." Jackson toyed with Alel's bottom lip, teasing him with soft, half kisses.

Alel moaned and his tail hit Jackson's calf a third time. He massaged Jackson's biceps. Their kisses built up steam as they shifted against each other. Alel muttered the word rosemary against Jackson's lips, and Jackson broke their kiss with a grin and a quick giggle before dipping his tongue into Alel's mouth. Alel whined in ecstasy. His tail wrapped around Jackson's waist. Jackson's shirt was bunched up from the way he lay, so Alel's tail happened to catch bare skin instead of cloth. Alel cried out; he clawed at the sheets and arched up. As soon as the fit passed, he grabbed his tail with his hand and yanked it away, holding it away from their bodies as if angry with it.

But Alel's skin against Jackson's back had been warm and pleasant. Jackson found himself missing the slender hugging sensation of it the moment Alel pulled his tail away, so he gently covered his hand over Alel's.

"You can wrap it around me."

"I'm...too..."

"It's okay." Jackson kissed him, slowly, deeply, sensuously. "You're making me feel good. Let yourself feel good too."

"But it's not the same kind of good," Alel muttered as Jackson unhinged Alel's fingers from his tail.

"It doesn't have to be. I told you it's okay if you come when we kiss." A wave of bashfulness swelled up in Jackson.

His voice dropped to a whisper. "It's actually arousing when you do."

Alel's panting grew desperate. He wrapped his tail back around Jackson and squeezed. Jackson sighed at the calming pressure around his waist. The hand holding the tail now braced the back of Jackson's head while Alel's other hand slid beneath his shirt and up his back. Jackson grabbed both of Alel's horns. Their lips kneaded together, occasionally interrupted by the slight flick of a tongue. After a few minutes, Jackson's hands unwound from Alel's horns and started to wander across his body. He slid his fingers beneath Alel's shirt and toyed with his smooth, flat belly. Alel's tail gave Jackson's waist a shuddering squeeze, relaxing a moment only to shudder tightly around Jackson's waist again.

Alel's hand on Jackson's back dropped to his ass. He pushed as he arched and moaned, but Alel only did this one time before deciding it was too much and moved his hand to its original spot on Jackson's back.

Jackson dropped down and sucked on Alel's dove-white throat until he decorated the creamy skin with beautiful splotches of red-violet. Alel arching into him until his cock pressed hard against Jackson's pelvis, had been thrilling but frightening. Part of Jackson wanted to push back, part of him wanted to pull away. Not knowing which urge to follow, Jackson was grateful when Alel stopped.

But he wanted to do something. He wasn't ready for grinding—not yet, maybe never or maybe after more time, Jackson wished he knew, himself—but he wanted to touch more of Alel, to make him cry out, to make Alel as happy as he was. His hands traced across Alel's body. They slid up and down his stomach, kneaded his chest, squeezed his shoulders, and as they dragged along Alel's belly, Jackson accidentally bumped his right hand against Alel's tail. Alel whimpered against Jackson's lips, knotting their legs together and squirming in an attempt not to hitch again. Jackson ran his palm over Alel's tail.

"Jackson!"

He pulled them onto their sides in order to reach the beginning of Alel's tail where Alel said it'd be most sensitive. Jackson enclosed his fist around the base and twisted with small strokes of his wrist.

"Oh my god!" Alel dug his fingers into Jackson's shoulder. "J-Jackson? Y-you don't mind?"

"I want to." The more Jackson looked into Alel's bright gaze and kiss-swollen lips, the more he wanted to see him come. Jackson kissed the side of Alel's neck, curving up his jaw to his ear before speaking in a low voice, "I want you to come while I hold you."

"Jackson…"

Now Alel hitched back instead of forward. His top wing lifted up in excitement while the bottom one spread out against the mattress. Jackson was tempted to lean closer and kiss Alel's wings, but they were more sensitive than Alel's tail, so Jackson held back.

"Oh God. Oh God. Oh-god-oh-god-oh-god!" Alel struggled with the button on his pants, shoving his hands down the front. "Nnnngh!"

Jackson held his breath, watching in fascination. His cock twitched at the needy sounds Alel made and the way Alel's tail whipped side to side in desperation while his wings fluttered.

"Aaaah! God, Jackson! God!"

Alel's muscles contracted. With a gasp, he crumpled in on himself. With a sigh, his tail and wings sank to the mattress, as slack as the rest of his body. He muttered something Jackson couldn't make out, but nevertheless, Jackson found himself kissing Alel's face.

"You're cute when you're excited." Jackson kissed his neck.

"It doesn't bother you? When I'm too aroused, and, uh, want to, you know."

"I'm turned on," Jackson answered.

"But...I can tell you don't want to have sex or even get a hand job... It's confusing me."

"Honestly, it's a little confusing to me too. I guess kissing's just too good." Jackson sighed. "I could touch myself again. It was good when we did it last time."

"Only if you *want* to." Alel pulled their chests together and ran his tongue along Jackson's bottom lip. "Either way, I'm going to hold you close for the rest of the night."

A deep, sensual shiver ran up Jackson's spine. He'd heard so many other lines this far into a relationship: *if you really cared you'd let me get closer; maybe those other guys couldn't satisfy you, but I know what I'm doing; don't be a snob; don't be a tease; don't act like you don't want it when your cock says you do.* Jackson had given up on relationships, hated himself for not wanting the guys who wanted him, wished he was "normal."

Alel held him, running fingers up and down Jackson's arms, and it felt *so good, so damn good.*

"This is what I want," Jackson gasped. "This is what makes me feel good. This. Hold me."

Alel kissed him again. "Let me wash up, and I'll come back and love you properly."

Jackson nodded as Alel rushed to the bathroom. Five minutes later he was back and scooping Jackson up in his arms. He circled his fingers all over Jackson's back. Sometimes he'd dip to Jackson's hips or up to his ribs; sometimes Alel kissed Jackson's forehead while he caressed him late into the night. Even as Jackson fell asleep, the soft little touches lingered against his skin, and damn it was good.

NABERIUS SHOOK BENEATH the covers. He'd never been sick before and hated it. He dozed, but couldn't rest well because of the chills and aches in his body. A soft, cool touch graced his forehead, and Naberius moaned in relief.

"You really are sick." The voice sounded like church bells.

"Where's Alel?" Naberius murmured. "Did he find you?"

"Yes. I'm sorry I've made things difficult for everyone. I'll be right back."

Naberius moaned when the angel left, but the angel returned a moment later with a cool cloth. Sariel bathed Naberius's face and ran cool fingers across his forehead.

"Will medicine help?"

"I don't think so," Naberius tried to sit up, but his body was tender and movement hurt.

"I'm so sorry. I'm so sorry." The angel's head hung low. Their hair dropped downward like golden honey. Despite the pain, Naberius reached up to touch the angel's lips with his fingertips.

"Don't frown."

The angel gasped at Naberius's touch. They parted their lips and bent lower toward Naberius. His hands moved to the soft, honeyed hair. The angel sighed and started to squirm, and then the angel pulled back. Naberius watched, afraid he'd done something wrong. But the flavor of savory candy filled the air, and Naberius licked his lips.

"I'm going to disrobe; tell me if it hurts you," the angel said. Naberius opened his mouth to ask why it would, but a bright light made him wince.

"Goddamn. Why didn't you glow last time?" Naberius shielded his eyes with his hand.

"The robe was around my waist, but...well, you see, an angel is never truly naked."

Naberius blinked until his eyes refocused. Tears trickled down the demon's cheek, but not because it hurt, and not because it was too bright. It had more to do with the emotions sparked by the divine light shining from the angel.

"Does it hurt you?"

"A little. I don't mind."

"May I approach you?"

Naberius beckoned the angel closer, and Sariel crawled onto the bed. Naberius lost himself at the sight. The angel was beautiful, beautiful, beautiful, with honey hair, and bright wings, and skin made of light.

"Unconditional love," the angel said. "That's why you're crying. It's new, isn't it? You've never known this feeling?"

"I know it." Naberius thought for a moment. "I've seen it in Alel. He dims it, though."

"Yes, I've seen his skin glow slightly even while wearing clothes, and he loves to caress his lovers and call them by name."

"He never was good at being an incubus. I had to drag him out for lunch all the time."

"I know." Sariel smiled as he started to undress Naberius. "He and I are friends because we're both awful at our jobs." The angel paused and blushed. "I wasn't over the other day to sleep with him. He let me borrow his apartment for the night. He was with someone else."

"Why does an angel borrow an empty apartment for a night?" Naberius watched, memorized, as the angel's white, nimble fingers undid his fly.

"I wanted to experiment...with touching my wings." Sariel continued to slowly undress Naberius.

"Did I interrupt?"

"No, I was sleeping by the time you showed up, but I was still worked up, so when you touched my back—"

"And then you kissed me."

"It was a reflex, but that's no excuse, and I'm sorry." Sariel slid Naberius's pants off, freeing his tail and ankles from the material before tossing them to the side.

"Is this part of the apology?" Naberius asked as the angel pulled his shirt up over his shoulders. Cool air caressed his fevered skin, but the angel's caresses felt better.

"I wanted more," the angel exhaled in frustration. Their gold hair and unconventional behavior reminded Naberius of Lucifer, of how he was once an angel. "I think demons should pray and kiss and love if they want to, and I think angels should curse and sleep and fuck if they want to."

"How? If you're not—"

Sariel grabbed Naberius's wrists and tugged them forward. His fingers plunged into snowy feathers, and he gasped. The texture was silky and addicting to touch. He found himself exploring and caressing every feather he could get his hands on.

"Shit," Sariel swore and held Naberius's shoulders for support.

The angel crawled into Naberius's lap, and Naberius grunted as his stiff dick rubbed against the angel's smooth belly.

"Touch me, please," the angel begged.

Naberius already was. He couldn't quit the luxurious act of petting through the silken feathers. He kneaded the top ridge and listened to the way Sariel's breath quickened.

"May I touch yours?" The angel asked.

Naberius spread out his wings. He grinned with pride when Sariel's eyes lit up at the sight of them.

"They're so big. They remind me of dragon wings." Sariel reached out and rolled their palm against the leathery undersides. "I really, *really,* enjoy touching them."

"Good."

Naberius leaned forward and pressed his face into the feathers behind Sariel's shoulder. He gave a sensual purr, and the angel moaned, pressing closer and sliding their body up Naberius's cock. Both the angel and demon flapped their wings at the same time, clashing together.

"Fuck. Oh fuck." Sariel gasped, grabbing Naberius's horns.

This time the angel restrained themself from kissing Naberius, but their mouth hovered close as Sariel moved up and down in Naberius's lap in order to cause friction against the incubus's cock. They both gasped, the tips of their wings continued to clash, sending jolts of pleasure through both of them. Naberius wrapped his tail around Sariel's waist. He tugged at the angel to encourage the grinding movement. Naberius spit on his cock to add a little lubricant.

"Gross." Sariel wrinkled their nose.

"Not as gross as tasting someone else's spit."

"To each their own." Sariel's breath huffed from their mouth.

Sariel tugged harder against Naberius's horns. Their mouths didn't touch, but each pant of air from the angel's mouth tickled his lips. Naberius's brain short-circuited. His fever chills were mixed with pleasure chills and he couldn't tell the two apart. Everything tasted of chili and lime and mole, so rich and filling and *good.*

"Do it." Naberius curled his fingers and yanked at the angel's feathers.

Sariel moaned at the rough tug to their wings. They gave Naberius a lust-glazed, questioning glance. Naberius's lips trembled. Was it the fever talking? No, he'd been thinking about this kiss since it happened, so filthy, so degrading, that it was a thrill. His binge eating, his fever, his chills, all happened because he was trying to deny his most base, primal desire.

"Kiss me."

"I-I don't think I should?"

"Why not?" Naberius squeezed harder with his tail and smacked his wings hard against the angel's.

"I don't want to hurt you."

"Sweet, little angel, hurt me all you want. I can handle it." Naberius kept his eyes open but lowered his bottom lip to tempt the angel.

Sariel scraped their teeth against Naberius's lower lip. He grinned through the erotic, violent gesture and licked Sariel's bottom lip in return. Their tongues bumped together. The warmth and texture startled Naberius. He jerked back, blinked at the angel, and lunged forward again. Sariel grabbed Naberius's cock and gave it continuous, fierce jerks with their hand. They pulled back, spitting against their palm and gliding easier afterward.

"It—should—be—disgusting." Naberius gasped ragged breaths between words. "So—why—is it—so—damn *hot* when you do—do it—oh God, I'm going to come!" His cheek landed onto a pillow of feathers, soft, soft, soft, and he moaned.

"It's warm!" Sariel shouted, withdrawing their spunk-coated hand. "Why is it so warm?"

"Because my body is warm." Naberius gave the angel a wicked, sleepy grin. "Lick it off of your hand."

"O-okay." Sariel's face was lovely as a rose: bright, red, dew-speckled, but their flush deepened as they shyly dipped their fingers into their mouth one at a time, sucking them clean.

Naberius rewarded the angel with a deep kiss, tasting himself. It was as if Naberius's most wild, secret, lewd, and seductive wet dreams all melted together in his fever heat.

"I didn't mind the taste," Sariel said, lips wet and gleaming.

"Neither did I," he answered, referring to kissing in general.

"I-I haven't—"

"How do angels finish?" Naberius asked, more than a little lost without a hole of some sort to shove his cock into.

"Touch my wings." Sariel nuzzled against Naberius's shoulder.

His breath caught. The little action was simple, and yet somehow it made Naberius yearn to please the angel in a way he never cared to do with a human. His fingers danced between feathers. He combed out the kinks and ruffles he'd made when yanking at them. Sariel leaned back, making a sultry noise an angel probably wasn't supposed to make. Naberius smoothed over the longer flight feathers and palmed at the smaller down near the base. Sariel called out in a long string of *ohs*. The angel's nails sank into Naberius's shoulders and bethe incubus grinned as he watched the angel unravel in front of him.

"Yes, yes, a...a little...more, please. Touch me! Ahh! Ahh!" The angel shuddered and convulsed and collapsed into Naberius's arms with a satisfied exhale.

"I got you," he whispered into the angel's hair. "I got you."

"Mmmm...sleepy," Sariel muttered.

Naberius pulled Sariel to his chest. He stroked Sariel's hair while keeping his tail wrapped around the angel's waist.

"Will the light bother you?" Sariel murmured while falling asleep.

"Bother me? No, but I'm surprised it doesn't burn me alive."

Chapter Nine

"FOLDING LAUNDRY IS my least favorite chore." Jackson bundled up a pair of socks and threw them at Alel.

Alel lifted his hand and blocked the socks. They hit his palm and bounced away. "Don't look at me. I'm better at taking clothes off than cleaning them and putting them away."

"How do you get the holes for your wings and tail?"

"I've gotten used to altering my own stuff."

"But how do you *fit* the wings."

"They're flexible." Alel noticed Jackson staring at them. "I'm, sorry...I'd let you touch them, but—"

"It's all right." Jackson's complexion hid his blush, but that didn't stop Alel from tasting fresh berries washed in summer rain.

He stared at the pile of towels beside him. He smelled fabric softener and cotton, and he focused on the scent to try to calm down from the strange energy in the air the last three times he'd visited Jackson. It seemed to be building with each new date they went on.

"Hey, let's go somewhere tonight. Let's go bowling."

"You don't want to stay home and watch a movie?" Jackson asked.

"We could." Alel folded another towel and set it in a neat square on top of the first. "Maybe we could—"

Jackson launched himself onto Alel. They collided, and Alel crashed against a pile of unfolded towels. Jackson's kisses were quick and frantic. Alel held his breath, surprised at first, but then he wrapped his legs around Jackson's waist. When their lips and tongues and hands couldn't work any faster, Jackson buried his face against Alel's chest. His body went slack, and he melted against Alel. Alel blinked and wondered what caused the burst of passion from Jackson. The mixed signals were confusing for Alel. He sensed Jackson *yearning*, but as always, it was more complicated than simple lust, so he wasn't sure what to do.

"Maybe staying home would be nice." Alel's fingers twined through Jackson's hair, mind racing for any idea to make Jackson happy. "We could do back rubs."

"Yes. Back rubs," Jackson said, excitement brightening his face. "Those will be nice after a day of the dullest chores ever."

Alel kissed Jackson's forehead and traced his cheekbones with his fingertips. Jackson's expression softened.

"I love you," Jackson whispered.

"I love you too." Alel kissed Jackson's forehead. He dug his fingers into Jackson's ribs, tickling him. "Don't make me fold all this myself. Get back to work."

Jackson screamed in laughter, rolling over and wrinkling the pile of shirts. He crawled back to his original spot and grabbed a pair of pants.

"Does this mean the honeymoon is over?"

"This *is* pretty domestic. It's a good thing the forces of hell are lazy because I can't imagine what they'd do if I was caught."

"They wouldn't...hurt you. Would they?" Jackson's brow creased, but his overall expression was hard to read and Alel wasn't sure if it was anger or concern lining his face.

Alel stared at his current towel. "What I'm doing...is treason."

"Because we're not having sex?"

"No." Alel couldn't help his gentle smile. "It wouldn't matter even if we were having sex. I love you. Love is treason because it's God."

"Then why doesn't God do something about it?"

"Hell, I don't know. Ask Sariel, but I doubt the angels know any more than the demons."

"If they ever hurt you... It's not going to happen." Jackson gripped the cloth in his hands until his knuckles became white capped. "Even after I die. I'd break out of heaven and fight hell itself."

Alel smiled but didn't respond because he knew better. It was still nice daydreaming about Jackson sweeping in, scooping Alel into his arms, and whisking him out of hell forever, but Alel knew if he ever got caught not even Sariel could help him.

"Finally. That took forever." Jackson changed the subject by laying the last folded shirt on top of the pile. "What do you want for dinner?"

"Pizza." Alel winked at him.

"Good choice. Why don't I get started while you put all this away?" Jackson rushed off to the kitchen.

"Did you stick me with the boring part so you can go cook?" Alel called after him.

"Hey, they're your clothes too. You should be happy I share drawer space with you."

"I'm here three or more times a week," Alel argued while scooping up piles of clothes.

"I know, and after only six months of dating. You're lucky I'm so fond of you. No one else has ever gotten drawer space."

Alel rolled his eyes, but his tail wagged happily as he walked down the hallway to put up their shirts and pants.

When he finished, Alel sat at the island counter while Jackson stuck a pizza in the oven.

"We should have folded the clothes in the bedroom. Took me three trips," Alel said.

"You're the one who dumped them onto the living room floor." Jackson set a timer.

Yes, because Alel was avoiding the bed. Jackson was wound up with sexual tension, but tension didn't equate desire, so Alel made no moves toward him. Still, it was hard on Alel, a weight crushing his chest. A knock from the door provided a reprieve from Alel's thoughts as he darted to open it.

"Sariel?"

"Is it a bad time?" The angel asked.

"No. Want dinner?"

"You don't mind?"

"Come in, Sariel!" Jackson called from the kitchen.

"Sariel isn't a vampire either. You don't have to invite them in," Alel teased as he walked back to his favorite seat.

"Hey, it was a reasonable misunderstanding." Jackson flipped him the bird.

"Am I missing something?" Sariel asked.

"Don't worry about it." Alel sat. "Is everything okay? If Naberius does *anything* wrong, I will personally—"

"I thought I was supposed to be your guardian angel, not the other way around." The angel smiled.

"Consider me your demonic guard dog."

"Naberius is clumsy and stupid—more so than you—and I'm very fond of him." Sariel blushed. "That's actually why I'm here. I was wondering if you guys would take me shopping? Naberius said he'd take me to a club, and I want to dress up. He already taught me how to wear a glamour, but I want to wear real clothing." The angel tugged at their white robe. "Instead of this."

"Wait a damn minute. Is he taking you to the club in the same way he used to take *me* to the club? Because we never went home alone."

"That's none of your business, Alel." Sariel fidgeted with the napkins sitting next to them.

"Pretty uppity talk for the angel who used to spy on me all the time."

"I wasn't *spying*. I was watching over you in case you needed help."

"That's what I'm trying to do!"

Jackson leaned over the island counter toward Alel. "I'm sure an angel can take care of themself. Especially if Naberius is as much a pushover as you."

"He's not horrible, but he's selfish," Alel said.

"A little, yes, but not half as much as you think. He acts worse around you to set a 'good' example for you."

"Well he could have lasted a little longer in bed," Alel muttered. "He always rushed through meals."

"He was afraid."

"Not of getting too close to the humans." Alel snorted.

"No, of getting too close to you." Sariel rested their hand on Alel's shoulder.

"You two seemed to talk a lot."

"I suppose." Sariel blushed.

"I'm glad." Alel gave Sariel's ribs a playful nudge with his elbow.

"We'll be happy to go shopping with you," Jackson spoke up to help them divert the conversation.

"Thank you," Sariel said.

They ate and took an Uber to Alel's favorite clothing store. He made sure his credit card was in his wallet because he knew the angel didn't have any money. When Alel looked up from his wallet, he stepped back. The wallet fell from his hands and landed on the sidewalk with a soft thud.

"You're a girl," he said. As soon as he said it, he shook his head and held up his hands as if to guard himself. "I mean, you're not, but—your glamour."

Sariel looked down and back up. "I can't be invisible if I'm going to try on the clothes, right? I thought it'd be a good time to practice using the glamour."

"Sure. But I've never seen you in a glamour, so it shocked me."

"I don't see much difference." Jackson shrugged.

And Jackson probably didn't see the difference. To him, Sariel would simply be someone beautiful to admire, and the angel looked almost the same. The only difference was they now appeared to wear jeans and a black T-shirt along with mascara. Alel stared at the small rise of breasts beneath the baggy T-shirt. He realized he'd always thought of Sariel as male despite *knowing damn well better,* and he did so because he *preferred* the thought of Sariel being male back when he pined for the creature.

"Is it wrong?" Sariel gave Alel a worried frown. "You're staring at me funny."

"You look great. I mean it. I just... I, uh... I think I just figured out that I'm more into guys." The words tumbled from Alel's mouth before he gave them proper thought.

"Good." Jackson gave Alel a playful slap. "You shouldn't be flirting with my guardian angel anyway."

"I haven't flirted with Sariel in weeks!" Alel laughed, still surprised with himself. The thought of *preference* was new to him. Incubi fed whoever desired them. *Choice* wasn't supposed to be a factor, and he slept with women sometimes, but as he thought back...

"Should I change it?" Sariel asked.

"No, of course not." Alel rubbed his forehead. "You're perfect. You deserve something better to wear to the club, though, so let's get you some proper gear."

"But this glamour's okay? As a woman?"

"You're perfect," Jackson repeated Alel's earlier statement.

"Thank you!" Sariel threw their arms around both of them. "All right, let's shop! I've never gone shopping. This will be fun."

The store was busy enough to shop without an assistant harassing them. Alel and Jackson picked out several outfits. They chose a little bit of everything from miniskirts, to dresses, to leather pants and halter tops and then found an attendant and waited for them to open one of the dressing room doors.

"Do I have to try on everything?" Sariel stared at the pile of clothes and leather in their arms.

"No, only what you think you might want to wear," Jackson said.

"Alel," Sariel whispered, "what about my wings?"

"I tried to get things with open backs, but just put it on the best you can, and I'll alter whatever you choose after we buy it."

"You know, on second thought, maybe I shouldn't bother doing this. I already own a phone, and an outfit would get me into more trouble—"

"Get in the dressing room, Sariel."

"Oh God, what am I getting myself into?" Sariel asked the ceiling as they disappeared behind the door.

"Are you okay?" Jackson asked the moment Sariel was out of earshot.

Alel let go of a stressed chuckle building up in his chest. "I feel dumb for ever pining over Sariel. We would have been horrible together."

"It happens to all of us. I have a few embarrassing high school crushes I'd rather not think about."

"I feel horribly human." Alel sighed, toying with his black ponytail to fidget with something.

"Is that so bad?" Jackson bumped him with his hip.

"It's strange. My whole life I never spent longer than a few weeks with any one person, except Naberius, but he was different because...well, it's hard to explain. Regardless, I never had a chance to consider what I wanted. What kind of relationship I'd *want* to have. What sort of person I'd *want* to date."

"What sort of person *do* you want to date?" Jackson asked, his face set in a careful, neutral expression.

Alel wound their fingers together. "You."

"Oh stop it." Jackson grinned and looked away, but squeezed their fingers together.

"It's not flattery," Alel said. "I've lived more in the last six months than the last thousand years."

"If you're trying to get smothered in kisses later—keep that sort of talk up."

"This one is my favorite!" The door swung open and an excited angel jumped out. Sariel had chosen purple leather pants and a black corset.

"Heels or boots?" Alel asked.

"What?"

"Your shoes."

"What's wrong with my sandals?"

"No, angel, no. Let's get you a pair of black boots to go with the corset. Do you want lipstick or no?"

"I...yes? So, um, do you think Naberius will like the outfit?"

"I think Naberius would think you were beautiful in a burlap sack." Jackson gathered up the extra clothes and placed them on a rack for unchosen garments. "Otherwise he's a complete fool."

"He's definitely a fool." Alel shrugged. "But your outfit is perfect, so don't worry about it."

"I can't thank you enough." Sariel wrapped both Jackson and Alel into a bearhug.

"Stupid angel." Alel mussed up Sariel's hair. "Let's pick out a pair of boots."

"WELL, THAT WAS an unexpected adventure." Jackson stretched and tilted from side to side once they were back in his apartment. "We helped an angel pick out club gear. Sariel looked so happy. More angels should get to go out on dates."

"Yeah…" Alel gave Jackson his sleepiest, come-hither stare.

"What's that face for?" Jackson grew bashful. He fidgeted with the hem of his shirt, a little smile playing on his lips.

"Oh, no reason." Alel walked toward Jackson, slow, intentional, seductive. He leaned close until their noses almost touched. "But if I remember correctly, I promised you a massage after dinner."

"Hmm," Jackson agreed with a hum and a single shake of his head.

"If you're ready, we can go to your room." Alel raised an eyebrow.

Jackson reached out, as if to touch Alel, but then jerked his hand back and marched to the bedroom. For a moment, Alel feared he'd come on too strongly, but when he entered the room, Jackson already lay on his stomach in nothing but a pair of boxers.

Alel stripped to his boxers as well. He grabbed a bottle of massage oil from a nearby shelf and crawled onto the bed.

He straddled Jackson's ass before settling into a comfortable position.

Alel lost himself in the experience. He smoothed the oil across Jackson's beautiful brown skin and allowed his fingers to wander wherever they wanted—lower back, spine, shoulders, neck. Jackson's skin was warm and soft and slick with oil and such a fucking delight to touch. Alel sighed in pleasure.

In order to drag the message out as long as possible, Alel continued down Jackson's arms, and calves, and even his feet. Jackson rewarded the attention with soft moans and subtle shifts of his body. Alel kneaded Jackson's skin until he couldn't take it anymore, and he leaned close and nuzzled against Jackson's wild hair. He meandered to Jackson's ear. He gave the outer shell a few playful nibbles and pressed lingering kisses into the un-oiled side of Jackson's neck.

"Alel, don't stop," Jackson begged.

Alel grinned through his kisses. He rolled Jackson onto his back so he could ravish Jackson's throat and collarbone with gentle nibbles and aggressive kisses. Jackson dug his fingers into Alel's ribs. The odd energy swelling between them intensified. It was *want* and it was *desire*, but it *still was not lust*, and Alel didn't know how to handle it, so he threw himself harder into each kiss. He put all his want and need and tension into the way his lips danced across Jackson's skin. Jackson's fingers twitched. They inched their way up Alel's ribs toward his back.

"Careful." Alel gasped when Jackson's fingers strayed too close to his wings. If Jackson's fingers got any closer to them, he was afraid of hitching from the pleasure, and he didn't want to make Jackson uncomfortable.

"I can't take it anymore," Jackson whispered, voice husky. He dragged his fingers along the folds of Alel's dark wings.

"Shit!" Alel screamed. Satisfaction rushed through Jackson, and Alel came quick and hard because of it. He gritted his teeth as he rode out the sharp, incredible shiver. "Oh shit."

Jackson flipped them. He scrambled over Alel and grabbed his box of tissues. Stripping the boxers from Alel's body, Jackson cleaned him up and started to kiss across his shoulder.

"Spread them," Jackson spoke against Alel's lavender-freckled shoulder as he reached up and undid the hair tie from Alel's hair so his now-long hair could spray across the pillows below him.

Alel almost spread his legs, too used to fucking while disguised in a human glamour, but part of his mind realized Jackson was talking about his wings. Alel stretched them out, covering the bed and extending past each side. Jackson stared, eyes gleaming. He brushed his fingers along the web-like patterns where the veins showed through the skin of the underside of his wing.

Alel arched his back, groaning. He shot Jackson a lidded stare, watching the way Jackson's face looked as he smoothed his hands out toward the tips and then back toward the center. Jackson lay so their chests pressed together. He leaned over and kissed along the upper ridge of Alel's right wing. Alel struggled to breathe, overwhelmed by Jackson's lips massaging his wings.

"They're smooth," Jackson said as his tongue traced along the slender "finger bones" of his right wing.

"I'm going to come again." Alel gasped.

"Is it that good?" Jackson's fingers spread wide and then swirled along the membrane of Alel's wing.

"When you do it, it is," Alel managed between desperate breaths.

"When I do it?" Jackson asked, his tone thoughtful. "What about when I do this?"

Jackson reached out and curled his fingers around Alel's cock. Alel whimpered, unable to hold in the noise as a jolt ran through him. Jackson stroked Alel's cock, his grasp firm. Alel's toes curled and come fountained onto his stomach. Jackson bit his bottom lip, looking pleased with himself, and Alel noticed Jackson's cock twitch through the fabric of his boxers. Jackson retrieved more tissues to wipe Alel dry.

"Please," Alel begged as Jackson cleaned him. Alel wrapped his tail around Jackson's waist, wrapped his wings around Jackson's body, and wrapped his arms around Jackson's neck.

"Don't stop."

"Mmmm." Jackson smiled, a shy and tentative movement of his lips. He grabbed Alel's still hard cock and stroked him a second time. Jackson moaned as he brushed his cheek against Alel's wing.

"Is this—what—you've been—wanting? The last few dates?" Alel panted as Jackson worked Alel's cock as if he owned it. "To touch my wings?"

"They're so smooth." Jackson moaned against them. "They flash in the light and they're so pretty. I've always wanted to touch them, but I knew they were private for you." Jackson kissed every inch he could reach. "But I couldn't take it anymore. I *wanted to know how they felt*, and I wanted to kiss them, and I wanted to hear you scream when I did it."

"Oh Jackson." Alel's mouth was agape as he struggled to breathe. He hitched into Jackson's palm, further aroused by Jackson's words. "This...so good, oh baby, please. More."

"How do I taste?" Jackson asked, stroking harder while licking across Alel's wings.

"Communion!" Alel cried out without thinking. His face burned hotter than hellfire, and a few strokes and kisses brought Alel to his third climax. Alel held his breath while he rode out the delirious pleasure.

"Communion?" Jackson asked after Alel finished. They lay bundled together. Alel's wings wrapped around Jackson in a needful embrace.

"I should not have said that. I-I shouldn't even know how communion tastes," Alel stuttered. "Maybe I don't really know, but that's how it *felt*."

"Do you mean bread and wine?"

"No, I mean something sacred. The kind of love I'd die to protect..." Alel closed his eyes. "I'm a little afraid. The more I'm with you, the more I love you."

"I won't let hell hurt you." Jackson kissed his chest.

"I'm not afraid of hell anymore, but this feeling—" Alel clutched his chest, right where Jackson had kissed. "It's so...bright."

"Alel I—I want to touch myself. Right now. With you watching."

Alel's eyes shot open. Jackson's eyes were dilated, his lips were plump, and his hair was bed-tousled. He was a delicious sight, a full-course meal from only a glance, but there was something more to it all, something beyond the need to absorb energy. Alel grabbed Jackson's face and kissed him and ran his fingers across Jackson's shoulders.

"I'd love to watch," Alel said, letting go with his hands and wings, but he kept his tail around Jackson to keep it still because he didn't want to stop to rummage for his "tail condom."

Jackson rose up. He sat straddled over Alel and slipped his hand down the front of his boxers. Alel rested his hands above Jackson's knees. He brushed his thumbs across Jackson's skin and squeezed with his tail, but otherwise didn't touch.

Jackson dragged his left hand along the front of his chest and down to his stomach. He ended by palming Alel's tail and making the incubus shiver. Jackson continued to rub Alel's tail with the palm of one hand while toying with his cock with his other hand. Alel would have loved to pull away the boxers so he could see Jackson's entire cock instead of the tip, but he figured Jackson kept them on intentionally, so he left them where they belonged. Little shivers skirted through Alel's tail to the rest of his body. Between Jackson's touch and the sight of him touching himself, Alel wanted to come again.

"If-if you keep touching m-my tail—"

"Still turned on?" Jackson stared at Alel with eyes darkened by arousal.

"You taste like steak, but dammit, you could be bland as saltine crackers and watching you would turn me on."

"Use your tail to get yourself off," Jackson said, breath hitching as he touched himself. His hips rocked as he thrust into his clenched fist.

Alel unwrapped himself from Jackson's waist. Since Jackson sat on Alel's stomach, there was plenty of room for him to coil his tail around his own cock and match his rhythm to Jackson's. They moved together, shifting and writhing in shared, individual pleasure. Alel sensed

Jackson's desire climb. The flavor of caramel filled his mouth, but he was only half aware of the flavor. He was too lost in the way Jackson's mouth twisted into a cute knot as he grew close to orgasm.

"Mmmm," Jackson moaned, his tone high and wanton.

"Yes," Alel encouraged twining his fingers with Jackson's free hand. "Keep going. I'm going to come when you do."

Jackson started bucking. His lips pursed and sweat made his brow shine. The tension stretched across Jackson's torso and emphasized the muscles in his arms and chest. Alel coiled his tail around his cock more tightly. He lifted his hips as his body spasmed.

"Alel, ahh, Alel I'm—" Jackson shrank in on himself, come staining the front of his boxers.

At the same time, Alel came. He leaked down his cock and onto his tail, and the orgasm felt like dawn breaking out past the horizon, bright and beautiful, causing gooseflesh to break out across his skin. Jackson curled against Alel's chest. Alel wrapped his wings around them, then sucked in a deep breath, satisfied and content.

"See why you have to help with laundry? My boxers are soaked through."

Alel laughed and stroked Jackson's hair.

"Are you happy?" Jackson asked.

"I'm always happy when I'm with you," Alel muttered. He could have never admitted it six months ago, but saying it to Jackson was easy now.

"No, I mean, was that enough? I'm, um, I don't know if I'll ever be ready for anything more, but I was hoping—"

"Jackson, you're beautiful." Alel pulled him closer for a kiss. "And I love you."

"Please, Alel, don't dodge the topic. I need you to be honest. Is this enough?"

"Jackson, I came four times! Although..." Alel blushed at the memory of Jackson with his hand down his boxers and his head thrown back in the final moment before coming.

"What is it?"

"It's better when you come too." Alel toyed with the tips of his unbound hair. "It's better because I feel we're...connected? Never mind, I'm being dumb."

"It's not dumb." Jackson nuzzled against Alel's sternum. "I agree, actually. That's why I wanted to touch myself...but, is it enough?"

Alel kissed Jackson's forehead. "If you have any doubts about whether or not you're doing enough—well, look at me!"

Alel couldn't see himself, but he could *feel* the difference. His wings were longer, as if they'd grown for the sole purpose of being able to better wrap around Jackson's body. Above all else, he felt like...an angel. He glowed—he was full of love—he'd never be able to return to hell again because he no longer belonged there.

"Oh! You're shimmering." Jackson touched Alel's face. "And your horns are fully curved now—and you have more freckles!"

"What? Really?" Alel examined himself. Extra flecks of lavender dotted against his chest. "Dammit."

"I love them." Jackson kissed up Alel's throat. His trail of kisses ended at the tip of Alel's nose. "I love you."

Chapter Ten

"HOLY SHIT. YOU look amazing." Naberius's mouth dropped when he saw Sariel.

"I know I'll be wearing a glamour, but this way, afterward—*eeee!*"

Naberius hoisted Sariel into the air and spun them in a circle. He set them down and grabbed two fistfuls of feathers.

"Afterward, I'm going to do this." He yanked, making Sariel flush and cry out. Naberius kneaded Sariel's wings until the angel writhed against him. "And I'm going to keep doing this until you can't stand it anymore."

"Let's stay home," Sariel begged. The angel ground their body against Naberius's cock.

"You said you wanted to try dancing." Naberius grinned like the devil he was, kissing up Sariel's jaw and dragging his fingers through more feathers.

"I do, but—your hands are so fucking good." Sariel bit Naberius's neck.

Naberius arched and gave Sariel's wings another tug. Their mouths crashed together, and they licked each other's lips as Naberius teased Sariel's wings. Then he slapped the angel's ass.

"Ah!"

"Let's go." Naberius activated his glamour and adjusted his hard-on in his jeans before turning to leave.

"Oh, you wicked, awful demon," Sariel slipped into their own glamour and followed Naberius out the door.

"Thank you."

"It *wasn't* a compliment."

"Yes it was, and you know it."

Sariel giggled. The angel laced their fingers with Naberius's.

"Are you all right?" Naberius asked.

"Y-yeah."

"Are you nervous about dancing?"

"No. I'm looking forward to it!" Sariel beamed, but then their face grew shy again. "I've been thinking a lot."

"About me, I hope." Naberius winked.

"In a way… I went shopping with Alel and Jackson. They helped me pick out the outfit."

"Remind me to send them a bottle of champagne to show my thanks."

"Alel called me a girl when he saw my glamour…"

"I'm sorry?" Naberius said it as if he wasn't sure if he were saying the right thing. "He was very insistent about me not calling you a girl after I first met you."

Sariel frowned, turning away.

"Hey." Naberius stopped the angel and tilted their face toward him. "Tell me."

"It made me happy," Sariel whispered, "when he said I was a girl."

"Girls wear braids and ribbons. You're a woman. Make sure Alel gets it right next time." Naberius pulled her closer, until their hips touched, and then started walking again.

"The glamour isn't real."

"Who cares? Do what you want, angel."

"Hmph, you're just saying that because you think it's cute every time I do something to piss off the other angels."

"I'd agree with you, but then I'd be telling the truth, and I should be lying instead."

"You're horrible." Sariel smiled as they continued walking. There was a line into the club, but Naberius ignored it. He walked right up to the front, winked at the bouncer, and walked through. Sariel blinked, confused. "Why didn't he send us to the end of the line?"

"Slept with him a few times."

"Pfff. You probably bribed him." Sariel laughed.

The neon lights inside somehow highlighted Naberius's smug expression. He pushed his way through the dance floor, held Sariel close, and swayed their hips. The music coursed through them, base pumping harder and faster than their heartbeats. Naberius leaned close and nuzzled Sariel's throat.

"One moment." Sariel pulled away and ran off into the crowd.

"We're on a date!" Naberius called after the angel. "Don't work!"

"I'll be right back!" Sariel called over her shoulder as she vanished deeper into the crowd and switched from glamoured to invisible.

A woman walked away from the bar. Sariel touched her shoulder, and she turned and grabbed her drink as if in second thought. Another girl stood in the corner and frowned, anxiety wrinkling her brow. Sariel touched her forehead, and her face softened. She bobbed her head with the music. Although she still wasn't brave enough to dance, she was at least less miserable.

Sariel *accidentally* bumped into a guy so he stumbled into the girl he was dancing with. They both flushed and giggled. Sariel wasn't supposed to physically interfere, but she was nothing if not a hopeless romantic. Next, she grabbed a guy's hand and reached it out toward his drunk friend in time to snatch away his car keys. Sariel ended in the men's room standing behind a man staring into the mirror. She wrapped her arms around him, but the man jerked back.

"I must be pretty fucked up," he said. Sariel winced. She hated it when people could see her despite being invisible.

"Fear not. I'm a drug-induced hallucination." Sariel stepped forward and rested a hand on the man's cheek. "And when your hallucinations start worrying about you, it's time to give up the drugs and change your life." Sariel kissed his cheek, wondering if, in the morning, he'd realize hallucinations didn't leave lipstick smudges.

The angel walked out of the bathroom and changed back into her glamour before finding Naberius. He rubbed his thumb below Sariel's bottom lip.

"Who'd you kiss?"

"A man in the bathroom."

"You screwy angels need to stop kissing everyone you see."

Sariel leaned closer. "But I'm looking at you right now."

"Well, maybe not *everyone*." They held each other. Sariel lost track of time as she laughed and moved until she was breathless.

"Dancing is fun!" Sariel giggled after several songs. "It's similar to sex with clothes on."

"I could make it more like sex."

"You brute! We're in public—oh my God, if you stop, I'll slap you." To anyone watching, Naberius appeared to innocently rub Sariel's back, but the angel gasped and groaned and pressed her face into Naberius's shoulder.

"Stop? Oh no. You see, you did good deeds during our date. It's only fair I sin and unravel an angel right here in front of everyone." Naberius kneaded Sariel's ass with one hand and her wings with the other as they continued to dance.

"Demons always...talk tough, but...when it comes to action...they tend to be lazy. Fuck, so don't, oh fuck—fuck—don't say anything else—ah! Please! More!"

Naberius laughed and danced and thumbed through Sariel's wings as the angel arched against him. When the next song played, he lifted Sariel into his arms and carried her to the nearest wall. Hidden in the shadows behind a veil of smoke, Naberius held Sariel with one arm, while the other hand pressed the angel's left wing flat against the bricks. He palmed the flesh beneath the feathers. Sariel wrapped her legs around Naberius and held her breath to keep from screaming.

"Close?" Naberius asked as he blew against Sariel's feathers.

They fluttered and settled back in place. Sariel bit her fist and moaned loudly, but the bass of the speakers hid the noise. Naberius nosed her fist out of the way so he could pluck a kiss from Sariel's painted lips, and he didn't stop until the lipstick was a memory and Sariel's nails dug into the incubus's shoulders. Sariel bit Naberius's lip, hard, as the angel climaxed with a violent shudder.

"What were you saying about tough talk and no action?" He asked once she opened her eyes again.

"Hmmm."

"I think you owe me an apology."

"I'll apologize as soon as we get back to your apartment." Sariel panted and ran a finger up the invisible edge of Naberius's left wing.

"Maybe we should go back now." Naberius grinned.

Sariel licked her lips. "Dance with me for one more song."

He set Sariel down and spun the angel. She laughed and leaned back in Naberius's arms. They dipped and when Sariel came up, she slung one arm around Naberius's neck and dragged the other one across his chest. She hooked her fingers at the edge of his jeans and tugged. Then Sariel slipped her fingers below Naberius's belt line, toying with his skin.

"Maybe I should return the favor here instead of waiting?"

"A little harder to hide, but I don't have a sense of decency when it comes to public affection."

"Hmmm, I think I'd prefer to have you on a bed. This isn't a good song, anyway. Let's go." They stared at each other, ready to head out the front door.

Sariel thumbed Naberius's cockhead, teasing him. His gaze locked with hers as he hitched into her touch

"Thought we were leaving?"

"Couldn't help myself. I'm ready when—" Sariel gasped when time slowed to a stop around her and the air grew bright. Smoke froze in air midswirl and refracted the growing light.

"Oh shit," Naberius swore.

"You need to go. Right now. Go before they see you." Sariel yanked her hand out of Naberius's pants and shoved at his chest.

"I'm not leaving you alone with one of *them*." Naberius hissed at the archangel walking through the door toward them.

"I'll be fine, but you have to get out of here." Sariel pushed Naberius harder, but he wouldn't budge.

"No."

"Step away." The angel stood tall with a spill of golden curls framing his shoulders and a robe so white it hurt to stare at even in the dark club lights. He pulled his sword and pointed it at Naberius.

"Make me." Naberius dropped his glamour and spread out his wings. His tail whipped in agitation as the angel approached.

"It's not his fault." Sariel dropped her glamour and jumped in-between the archangel and Naberius. "This is my sin—and my punishment—not his."

"You're an angel not a harlot." The angel sneered. "What have you been doing with this demon?"

"She'll dress however the fuck she wants!" Naberius growled. "You better leave or I'll—"

"Naberius, stop!" Sariel hung her head. "I deserve this. I knew I was breaking the rules—"

"No, don't you dare, this bitch isn't God, and I'm sick of archangels flying around telling everyone what to do. They're no better than the Sins. Fuck both sides! We're not doing anything humans don't do all the time."

"Sariel, we're going Home," the angel said.

"Home?" Sariel perked up, an involuntary smile gracing her lips. "I haven't seen Home in thousands of years." Her face dropped. "But what about—"

"The demon dies."

"No! You can't!" Sariel cried out.

"He's seduced one of our own. We can't allow him to live."

"Bring it. I'm not afraid of one punk-ass bitch angel."

"He didn't seduce me! I seduced him!" Sariel stepped back. She laced her fingers with Naberius's. "He was sick. I took advantage of him."

"Sariel, that's not what happened," Naberius growled.

"Yes it is," she insisted.

"You? You *initiated* carnal acts with a demon?"

"No." Naberius pulled his hand away. "I started it all. Take her home and fight me."

"He's a demon and he's lying." Sariel clenched her hands into fists. "It was my fault, so let him go."

"Sariel," the angel spoke in a quiet voice. "If you're the one who seduced him, you know I'll kill you both. There is no sparing a demon."

"What about mercy?"

"Mercy is for humans."

"I can't live knowing he died because of me, so the Lord's will be done." Sariel sniffed. Tears lined her eyes but didn't fall.

"Fuck the Lord's will—run!" Naberius grabbed Sariel's hand and pulled her around the angel and out of the club.

ALEL AND JACKSON stood in their secret cove of trees along the walking trail. With his wings larger, Alel could hold Jackson in his arms and cocoon them in a dark embrace without worrying about accidentally rubbing against Jackson and getting too worked up. Ever since Alel's last visit, the strange tension making Jackson uncomfortable had eased, and Alel thought it was endearing, and flattering, that Jackson had wanted to touch his wings so badly.

Alel had his arms around Jackson as well, and they brushed noses and nuzzled against the sides of each other's faces. Alel loved the warmth of their pressed chests and encircled arms and Jackson's breath tickling his cheeks.

"Stop or I'll kiss you," Jackson threatened with a giggle and hint of his lips dragging up Alel's neck. Alel shuddered, lost in the moment, lost in the warmth, lost in the joy he felt whenever he got to hold Jackson.

"Kiss me," he begged, lips parting and tingling in anticipation.

Jackson held Alel's face, bringing their mouths together in slow motion, driving Alel crazy. Their lips ghosted against each other. Alel closed his eyes and surrendered himself to Jackson's leisurely pace. They took their time exploring each other's lips. Alel took Jackson's hands and kissed his knuckles and wrists. He flicked his tongue against Jackson's pulse and grinned when Jackson's breath hitched. Their mouths met again, and their tongues flicked at each other before deepening into slow French kisses.

A scream broke the moment. They both jerked, and Alel curled his arms around Jackson to protect him. Alel's heart pounded. He tried to look around, but the trees protecting them also blinded them.

"Stay here."

"Alel, no."

But Alel was already peeking out from behind the pine trunks in order to view the street. His stomach sank when he saw Sariel and Naberius sprinting down the sidewalk with an archangel chasing them. Sariel tripped on their boot heels—heels Alel had insisted the angel wear—and Naberius dropped to his knees. He shielded the angel with his own body as the archangel unsheathed his sword.

Alel didn't have time to think. He flew—human viewers be damned, he didn't have enough time to run, so he flew—and blocked the sword stroke with the top ridge of his wing. The sword clanked as if it struck a shield. Sparks flew at the impact. The strike sent an unpleasant jolt through the nerves of Alel's wings, but he clenched his teeth, refusing to back down.

"How?" The angel stepped back, mouth agape.

"Alel? Is it really you?" Naberius asked.

"Alel!" Sariel shouted from the sidewalk. "Holy shit, you're glowing—you look like an angel."

Somehow, even in the middle of a fight, the statement made Alel blush. He knew it was true. It had to be. Nothing resisted the blade of an archangel, nothing except the feathered wings of Lucifer himself. Alel wondered exactly how strong he'd become if even an angel on par with Michael and Gabriel couldn't hurt him.

"What are you doing to my guardian angel!" Jackson sprinted to the middle of the fray. He pounded his fists against the archangel's chest.

"Jackson, stay back!" Alel pulled Jackson away.

"What is a human doing here?" The archangel asked.

"I...he was with me." Alel didn't trust the archangel. Alel got a strange vibe from him, as if the angel wanted to take his time hurting Alel—for pleasure, not for duty.

"He should have gone into suspension with the others." The angel said, giving Jackson a suspicious stare.

"Are you okay?" Jackson ignored the angel while helping Naberius and Sariel to their feet.

"Alel, take Jackson home. He shouldn't see this," Sariel pleaded.

"We can't leave if you're in trouble." Jackson glared at the archangel. "Don't angels have better things to do than ruin everyone's date night? Go save some orphans and leave Sariel alone."

"Let's examine your soul, human." The angel walked up to Jackson, who stood fearless, despite the creature's golden glow and gleaming sword.

"Don't." Alel jumped in the way.

The angel held up a hand as he stared at Alel. "I don't know how you've grown this strong but stand aside."

"If you hurt him—"

"You needn't fear. If he's committed no sin, there'll be no punishment."

Jackson matched the archangel's gaze, angry but silent. After a moment, the angel blinked and lowered his head in thought.

"The demon hasn't corrupted your soul."

"Alel corrupt my soul? Are you joking?" Jackson scoffed.

"But the human has corrupted mine." Alel snorted, angry at the way the angel talked as if he wasn't standing right there. Alel rubbed the spot on his wing where the sword hit. "I love him."

"Alel, shut up. You're lying." Naberius dug his talons into his palms as he spoke to the angel. "This dumb, human piece of cherry pie doesn't have sex, and Alel wanted a challenge, so he's lying and pretending to be lovesick. It's an act. Alel, tell them. Tell them you're faking. Tell them you're manipulating the human to fuck him."

"Naberius, you can see me. I'm glowing. I'm closer to an angel than a demon at this point."

Naberius ground his teeth and clenched his fists harder. "And are the angels going to protect you when Lust finds out you've betrayed hell? No. They're not, because it doesn't matter how much you glow. You're a demon, Alel! Act like one!"

"I am a demon." Alel dropped to his hands and knees. "And I'm giving up all my pride and begging, *begging* you, angel, to spare their lives. Naberius and Sariel are my friends, and I'd do anything to keep them safe. Please, spare them."

"Alel, you get up right now!" Naberius jerked him to his feet. "We do not bow! We do not beg! We do not love! Stop it!"

But a thin grin cut across the archangel's face. Alel sensed a dangerous sort of lust rise from the creature. It wasn't sexual, not directly; it was a lust for power, and seeing Alel beg had stroked the heat of it to a frenzy; so much so, Alel hugged himself in a vain attempt to find protection from the greasy coating it left on his tongue.

"Prove your side is better. Even demons kill their own for breaking the rules—show them mercy instead."

"Since you set aside your sinful pride for them, I'll let them live, but not without some sort of repentance." The angel folded his hands behind his back and turned his head to Sariel. "Repent and come Home with me."

"I want to stay." Sariel shook, clinging to both Jackson and Naberius.

The archangel scowled. "If you stay here, it will be forever. You will never be welcomed in heaven again."

Silent tears spilled down Sariel's cheeks, staring at the cracks in the sidewalk as if the light from the archangel was too bright to bear.

"Take her!" Naberius shouted. He pushed Sariel toward the archangel. "She belongs in heaven! Not here!"

"I don't want to leave you." Sariel stumbled and stared at Naberius with a wounded expression. The only reason the angel didn't fall was because Jackson caught them.

"Well, who said I wanted you!" Naberius screamed, loud and shrill. "I don't! I-I was using you! In the same way Alel is using Jackson! Don't you fucking idiots realize you're food? Neither of us care! Now run home, you stupid angel. I'm bored with you!"

Naberius's face burned crimson all over. He backed up several steps and turned to run, but Sariel dashed toward him and blocked his path. The angel shoved his chest, feathers scattering with the impact of the push.

"Don't you dare lie to protect me! I'm not Alel! And your tough demon act almost killed him! He was starving to death! Literally! But look at him now! Look! At! Him! That's Alel, Naberius, the real Alel. The Alel he never got to be because he never dared to break all of these stupid fucking rules we follow! Let him love Jackson! It makes him happy, you stupid demon! And you make me happy, so let me make my own choices!"

"There's no choice," Naberius growled. "You don't choose a demon over heaven—you don't!"

"You don't tell me what to do either!"

"I'm not telling you what to do. It's common sense! Dammit, Sariel, go Home!"

"No! I'm staying here!"

"Why? I'm not that great!"

"But potato chips are!" Sariel shouted the last line as loudly as the others.

It sounded so ridiculous they both stopped and hugged each other and laughed against each other's shoulder. They squeezed together, their affection for each other obvious in the way their fingers dug into each other, showing their fear of being separated. Around them, the world stood frozen. Cars sat in the streets, a bird hovered midflap in the air, even the stars seemed painted onto a black backdrop, bright and white, but not twinkling. The archangel currently had his fist clenched around the arrow of time itself, and it seemed wrong to Alel a single archangel could stop the world so easily.

"Snacking behind my back?" Naberius chuckled into Sariel's hair.

"We agreed at the beginning of this relationship we could have the occasional snacks on the side as long as we ate meals together."

"Are potato chips worth never seeing Home again?" Naberius asked, dropping the innuendo.

"I can't be female in heaven, and I can't bake cookies with Alel and Jackson, and I can't dance with you." Sariel turned to the archangel. "I'm sorry. I know I'll always yearn for Home, but I would rather be an exile, please."

"Are you sure?" The archangel's face twisted in anger at the entire, ridiculous scene. "You cannot make amends 500 years from now when you grow tired of playing with demons and mortals."

"God hasn't grown tired of humans after all these years. Why should I?"

"Enjoy reaping what you sow." The curly haired angel turned away, facing Alel. "I have questions for you."

"Leave him alone!" Jackson wrapped his arms around Alel, wings and all.

"Jackson, my wings," Alel whispered, flushed from both the touch and everyone watching as Jackson grabbed him.

"Sorry." Jackson moved in front of him instead. "But I'm not letting this jerk anywhere near you."

"It's all right. Ask your questions." Alel pulled Jackson into his chest and used his wings to protect them both.

"How can the human move?" The archangel asked a second time. "I've frozen time."

"I don't know. It's probably because we're together," Alel answered to the best of his ability. "We were standing together when you stopped everything."

"And even now you protect this human with your wings. Why?"

"Because I love him."

"You keep saying that, but you're an incubus."

"I am."

"Demons can't love."

"That's a lie. That's always been a lie."

"Look at him," Sariel said. "He's shimmering."

"Why does it make you so angry?" Jackson asked as he stared at the archangel.

"He's an incubus." The words flew with such vehemence from the archangel's mouth that Alel pulled Jackson a step farther away.

"He's angry because Alel is stronger than him." Naberius glared at the angel. "He's angry because he wouldn't mind seeing Alel on his knees again, and he's guilty for it, so he's lashing out."

"Demon, you lie," the angel snapped. "I'm angry because incubi are pests. Pawns that the Sins use to manipulate humans." The archangel pulled out his sword. "They're not strong enough to withstand our blades."

"Jackson, go make sure Sariel isn't hurt."

"Sariel is fine," Jackson grabbed Alel's wrist so they couldn't be separated.

"Go, Jackson. He can't hurt me, so don't worry."

It was Naberius and Sariel who came and pulled Jackson away. He fussed but, more or less, allowed himself to get towed back. Meanwhile, the archangel attacked. Alel sidestepped when he could, moving with a fluid, surprising grace. When he couldn't dodge an attack—he blocked with his wings. The more the angel fought, the more he snarled and swung without thinking, furious a low-class demon was dodging and blocking without any struggle at all.

"Stop it!" Jackson screamed. "He isn't evil! What's the point in fighting?"

But the archangel didn't listen. Finally, Alel slapped him with his tail which sent the fight to a sudden, shocked halt. The angel held his cheek. By the disbelief and hurt in his eyes, one would think Alel had stabbed him.

"There's no barb anymore." Alel lifted his tail to display the violet-black fringe similar to the tip of a zebra's tail.

"Alel, how the hell?" Naberius asked in a loud voice.

"I, uh, think it changed because I didn't want to poke Jackson when we cuddled?" Alel shrugged. It was a little embarrassing to talk about cuddling right in front of an archangel, but Alel refused to hide it anymore. He enjoyed cuddling. Fuck the archangel.

"That's not possible." The angel bared his teeth as he spoke, eyes wide in fury.

A frustrated huff left Alel's mouth. "Shouldn't you be happy? In a way, you won. I'm useless. Maybe I was only a pawn, but I'm off the board now." He gestured to Sariel and Naberius. "We're all off the board, okay? We want to eat pizza and go bowling. I mean, have you ever actually sat and *watched* a Vincent Price movie? They're amazing. Life is so much more than the petty things we make it. Please, I'll get on my knees again if that's what it takes, but please leave us alone."

"You're all dissenters of the cause." The archangel pressed the blade of his sword below Alel's jawline as he leaned in close. "Make no mistake, this battle isn't over."

"I don't want to fight you." Careful not to cut his neck on the sword's edge, Alel's gaze shifted to Jackson. "I only want to love him."

"Demons don't deserve love."

The archangel disappeared, and the world crashed back into motion. Cars roared to life, the bird overhead started to flap his wings again, and a leaf trapped in a current fluttered next to Alel's feet. Alel slipped back into his glamour before anyone could see him.

"You look amazing!" Sariel ran up to him and flung her arms around his neck. "And you made such a heroic entrance! Blocking an archangel's *coup de grace* at the last second. It was better than a movie scene."

"Didn't it hurt? With your wings?" Jackson asked.

"Wasn't pleasant, but objects don't feel the same as a touch, so it wasn't as bad as getting stabbed in the nuts." He turned toward Sariel. "How'd you piss off an archangel in the first place?"

"He burst into the club!" Sariel pouted. "Just when we wanted to leave."

"Was he searching for you?"

"I think so." Sariel sighed. "I...encouraged some people in the club. No miracles. A few simple nudges in better directions only, but I must have altered something enough to catch the attention of the archangels."

"See kitten, being good causes trouble." Naberius glared at Alel. "It's a good lesson for you to learn too."

"I'll keep it in mind. Anyway, since you're here, do you want to go bowling with us?" Alel asked.

"I've watched humans play, but I've never bowled myself." Sariel smiled.

"And I've never dragged an angel into the bowling alley bathroom to have my way with her. Let's go." Naberius licked his lips.

"Try that nonsense in the middle of our game and we'll throw gutter balls during your turn," Jackson warned.

"So, we should use she and her now?" Alel asked Sariel.

"You said it the other day." She gave him a shy smile. "It was nice, and the more I thought about it, the more I warmed to the idea of being referred to as a girl all the time."

"If you ever want to go shopping again, let us know." Jackson grinned.

"There were a few dresses I didn't buy last time but were nice." Sariel's wings fluttered in excitement.

"Grab Naberius's credit card, and we'll get you all the dresses you want." Alel led them down the street.

"Are you worried? About the archangel's threat?" Sariel asked.

"What's he going to do? Cry to God because a demon isn't running around and causing people to sin? He's mad and power hungry, but there's not much he can do if I'm not causing trouble."

"I still don't believe you slapped an archangel with your tail." Naberius winked. "That was pretty hot."

"He also folds laundry." Jackson threaded his fingers with Alel's as they walked. "He's pretty much the best."

"You're a horrible influence on me." Alel bumped Jackson with his hip.

"On all of us." Naberius sighed. "I can't believe we're going bowling. It's so... platonic. I would fly us out to Tahiti on the next available flight if you'd all agree to an orgy."

"I'd rather go bowling." Jackson snorted.

"I'd rather go bowling too." Alel shrugged.

"Quit kissing up to your boyfriend." Naberius frowned. "We've been to Tahiti plenty of times together."

"True." Alel scratched his arm. "But I never truly enjoyed it. I mean, it was fun enough at the time. Yet now that I know I have more options, I'd rather walk the beach and fool around in a hotel room. Sex on the beach gets sand everywhere, but the bowling alley has air conditioning and Jell-O shots."

"What's a Jell-O shot?" Sariel asked.

"Oh Sariel." Jackson grabbed her hand as they walked side by side. "We are going to have a fun night. And I suppose Alel and I *could* take a break between games to play air hockey if you and Naberius really do want to take a bathroom break."

"I do owe him." Sariel threw a coy glance over her shoulder. "So I might take up your offer for a break."

Chapter Eleven

JACKSON NIBBLED AGAINST Alel's bottom lip. He trembled beneath Jackson's weight, his tail sliding against the silk of Jackson's boxers. Jackson moved over to the other side of Alel's mouth as one hand tangled in Alel's hair and the other twisted the bud of Alel's nipple.

"Bet you're eager to finish," Jackson whispered in a deep, husky tone.

"Please," he begged, his tail flicking in excitement.

"Use your tail as I watch."

Jackson leaned back, and Alel roped his tail around his cock. His swollen tip slipped in and out of the coil of his tail, making Alel whimper. Jackson crawled over to the side, grabbing their bottle of lube and drizzling cold gel on Alel's burning flesh. Alel squealed as the cold hit his skin, stroking faster with his tail to warm the lubrication.

"How many orgasms does this make?" Jackson asked.

"F-five," he gasped, too on edge to speak more than single syllable words.

"And you said you can go until I'm satisfied?"

Alel nodded his head as quickly as he stroked himself.

"Hmmm... I want to touch myself, but..." he licked Alel's nipple. Alel called out and Jackson grinned. "I think I'm going to have to wait until you come a few more times."

"Jackson," Alel moaned as he climbed higher.

"I love how bright you glow when you're aroused." Jackson kissed along the trails of lavender freckles winding across Alel's body.

He arched into Jackson's kisses while panting and hitching his hips up and down. Jackson traced his fingers over Alel's chest and kissed up Alel's elflike ears. He always stopped to nibble at the sensitive tip, and when Jackson started to flick his tongue instead of bite, it was too much, and Alel splashed come all over his stomach.

Jackson dried him off and nestled back on top of him. Their tongues slid against each other as they kissed. Jackson traced the arch of blush on Alel's cheeks with the sides of his thumbs. His touch was cool on Alel's burning skin. Alel held onto Jackson's waist and focused on the way their lips brushed together.

Jackson's breathing grew heavy as his own arousal continued to climb. It was blueberry stilton and champagne, fresh loganberries picked after a summer rain, chocolate mousse spiked with Frangelico, and it was none of those things all at once. It was the taste of Jackson—of Jackson's lips and the sweat from Jackson's throat against Alel's tongue when their kisses moved to their bodies instead of their mouths.

Alel was confused. At some point, he'd stopped feeding off of Jackson's energy. It made sense...he'd climaxed five times, he was probably full? Although, he never heard of a demon being sated. Jackson moved up to Alel's wings. He'd been ignoring them, but now his tongue traced the thin wing bones and his lips graced across the taut, stretched skin.

"Don't stop. Don't stop. Please, Jackson."

"I won't stop," Jackson whispered against Alel's wings before trailing the shapes of hearts with his tongue along the underside of Alel's right wing.

Alel was touching himself again. He couldn't help it when Jackson wrote love notes with his tongue all over Alel's body. After about five minutes, he came yet again, with a strangled groan, and had to lie in bed a moment gasping and staring at the ceiling.

"Are you tired?" Jackson asked. He looked gorgeous in the dim bedroom lights.

"Don't stop," Alel begged.

"Let's come together this time." Jackson kissed the spirals of Alel's horns and squirmed lower so he could trace Alel's lips with his fingertips.

Alel's breath caught in his throat. He nodded and parted his lips as he savored Jackson's fingers tracing over his mouth. Alel sat up, holding Jackson in his lap. Jackson slipped his hand down the front of his boxers. His eyelids drooped low, and his gaze lost focus as he touched himself. Alel grabbed the lube and offered it to Jackson. Jackson nodded and pulled the band of his boxers out so Alel could drizzle the lube on Jackson's cock. Alel's eyes dilated. It was always a treat when he got to stare at Jackson's member, fat and long and the loveliest shade of brown. He took his time dripping the lube before setting the bottle aside and grabbing his own piece. Alel leaned forward and peppered Jackson's chest with kisses.

Jackson flexed; his muscles rippled against Alel's lips. Their breaths were loud in the quiet room and the bed creaked with their movement. Jackson shut his eyes, but Alel kept his open. He didn't want to miss the way Jackson's brow wrinkled or the way his lips puckered as he drew close to climax. Jackson's mounting pleasure radiate from his body in hot waves. Alel used the sensation to bring himself to the brink. Alel hovered and hovered. He dragged out the moment until a strangled cry erupted from Jackson's throat. Then Alel knew it was time, and he allowed his come to spill over his hand even as Jackson did the same.

"You just...keep going, don't you?" Jackson stared at the mess Alel made of himself. He eyed Alel's hard cock with curious fascination.

"I can't help it, I—"

Jackson interrupted Alel with a kiss. When they broke the seal of their lips, Jackson lowered the band of his boxers and angled himself toward Alel.

"Um..." Jackson grew bashful. Alel gazed into Jackson's eyes. He thought he knew what Jackson wanted, but had to be absolutely sure. "If, if you want, you, um, can..."

"You—you want me to?"

Jackson gave him a shy nod of consent, so Alel eased Jackson onto his back. He hooked his fingers around the band of Jackson's boxers and looked up at him. Jackson gave him an eager nod. Alel pulled Jackson's boxers all the way off. He grabbed the base of Jackson's half-hard cock and started to lick the come from Jackson's last orgasm off his shaft and tip. Jackson gasped and fisted the sheets below.

"How is it?" Alel asked between kisses to Jackson's shaft.

"G-god," Jackson whispered in a breathless voice.

Alel licked all the way up Jackson's shaft and kissed the tip. He repeated the action three times before kissing his way back down. Jackson's cock started to grow again, getting a little harder with each kiss.

"Alel, um, could...could you..."

"Yes?"

"Um, take it all the way into your mouth?"

Alel's heart leaped in his chest with excitement.

"God, yes I will." And that was the last Alel spoke. He sealed his lips around Jackson's shaft and swallowed him to his base.

After a few minutes of sucking, Jackson was fully hard. Alel tried to lap his tongue against Jackson's shaft, but he didn't have enough room with Jackson's girth filling his mouth completely. So Alel bobbed his head. When he went down, he went down deep. Alel relaxed his throat and took Jackson in all the way. He continued to move his head, enjoying the moment, never tiring of his rhythm or Jackson's breathing or the bed's creaking. Alel's tail wagged, and he was too happy to stop it from swishing in the air as he continued to suck on Jackson's cock.

"Alel!"

The Incubus wanted to moan and call out Jackson's name, but all he could do was breathe, and suck, and try to keep his excited heart from bursting through his chest.

"Mmmm, Alel." Jackson groaned.

His hands jumped from the sheets to Alel's hair. Jackson used the long, black strands like reins, controlling Alel's pace and depth with tugs and yanks, and Alel loved every second of it. He loved the smoothness of Jackson's cock in his mouth, and he loved Jackson's fingers pulling his hair, but more than anything, he simply loved how it was Jackson he was with. Alel couldn't imagine being with anyone else, and again, he thought one day he'd break into heaven for no other reason than to find Jackson and steal a kiss.

"God, Alel! Oh my God!"

Jackson hooked a leg over Alel's shoulder. Alel slipped his tail between his legs so he could use it to massage Jackson's balls while he continued to suck. He'd never had a chance to make love in any way without a glamour, so he never got to use his tail. The thought made him giddy. Alel spread out his wings and sucked faster and continued to use his tail to help pleasure Jackson, who screamed in ecstasy. Jackson made a sound that was probably a warning lost in pleasure as Jackson came into Alel's mouth. He swallowed and swallowed again, pulling free and sighing in contentment.

"Alel, I can barely see." Jackson laughed and shielded his eyes.

"Huh?" Alel blinked; he didn't understand.

"You're glowing as bright as a sunrise."

Alel blushed, staring at his arms. He wasn't sure *how* he was doing it. Somewhere in the back of his mind, he remembered Naberius mentioning Sariel had the same problem with she was naked, so he wiped himself off as quickly as possible and then wrapped himself in a blanket. The room dimmed the moment the fabric enclosed around his body.

"Sorry," he muttered, embarrassed.

"It's not supposed to happen, is it?"

"I, uh, think it happens to angels."

"Your wings are better." Jackson pushed himself up so he could kiss the tip of Alel's wings. Jackson giggled into the kisses. "I've never had two orgasms. I never wanted more than one before."

Alel sighed, thoroughly ravished after eight orgasms. Jackson's kisses were tender and sweet instead of arousing. He held Jackson a little closer.

"Want a nap?" Alel asked.

"Are you trying to cuddle with me?" Jackson grinned.

"Yes." Alel pulled Jackson against his chest and lay them both on the bed. He smothered Jackson's face with kisses. "I always want to cuddle. What do you want for dinner tonight?"

"Lasagna?"

"Sounds great. I'll make it after our nap."

"I love you." Jackson giggled at the barrage of kisses and bumped their noses together.

"Love you too." Alel's tail tried to wag again, but he had it trapped in the blanket.

They bumped noses again and giggled and squeezed each other close. The blanket slipped free and Alel lit up the room enough to make the dust motes glow around them. He covered himself again and dozed in Jackson's arms, but each time his beloved stirred, Alel became hyperaware of being held, and he'd get so happy his heart would flutter and he never quite made it to full unconsciousness. After a few hours, he decided to get up and cook dinner. Alel showered and dressed and sang to himself in the kitchen. As Alel bent over to pull out the lasagna, a sleek human shape—but not human—caught his eye. The entity sat cross-legged on the island counter.

"Lust?" Alel fumbled with the pan and managed to set it onto the counter without dropping it. He flung his oven mitts and prostrated himself on the kitchen floor.

"Smells delicious." Lust smiled. The Sin wore candy-red lips and a tight red dress, but the outfit wasn't a statement of femininity so much as a symbol of objectification.

"Great way to seduce humans into bed." Alel tried to laugh, but he'd lost the ability to lie somewhere along the line when he was learning how to glow.

"Surely. How many?"

"I'm sorry... I don't—"

"How many times have you used this trick to seduce a human?"

"Oh, you know...lots."

"Come here, Alel."

His stomach sank. The Sins did not use the names of lower demons, nor did they pop in for unexpected visits like a meddlesome mother. Alel's face flushed with anger as he walked forward.

"Did the archangel snitch on me?"

"Envy, another fine sin. The angel was jealous of your strength. He wanted your power, and he wanted to subjugate you, but those desires are unbecoming of an angel, so he came to me. I didn't believe the stories about a mere incubus who blocked an archangel's sword." Lust grabbed Alel's chin with their entire hand and moved his face from left to right. Lust's nostrils flared as they snorted. "But clearly, you're no longer a child of mine."

"Good. I don't want to belong to you. I hate you," Alel said the words with the casual disdain that only the condemned could use. He knew any happiness he had with Jackson was over, and he'd never experience anything but agony from this moment on. It was only a matter of how to protect Jackson. Making a deal with Lust would be futile. Praying to Sariel would probably get her killed.

God...

Lust slapped Alel. The red-leather glove they wore made the smack sting, and Alel's cheek burned long after the blow.

"Don't," the Sin hissed. Their breath, sulfur and Goldshlager, violated Alel's personal space.

"Or what?" Alel asked.

"I'll make you watch as I hurt him."

"I can destroy you," Alel whispered. "Don't confuse my love for the human with weakness. I will fucking destroy you if you don't let him live."

Lust laughed, licking red lipstick from their lips. Alel gave them a tight-lipped smirk and pulled his shirt up over his head and horns.

"Stripping. Is this a seduction?" Lust leaned back, amused. "You're pretty, but not as pretty as me."

Alel didn't answer. Instead, he used his thumb to pop open his pants and pull the zipper down. He slipped them off and let them pool to the floor. Uncovered, he thought of Jackson, of kissing him, simply kissing him. The old taboo that once terrified Alel now drew light from Alel's midsection, and the kitchen flashed white.

A shriek, and the Sin was gone, but Alel knew he had only bought a moment of time. He threw on his boxers and pants and ran to the bedroom to check on Jackson.

"Jackson!" he screamed as he slammed through the bedroom door.

Jackson yawned and stretched, oblivious to anything wrong, and it tore Alel's heart that he was about to ruin their contentment. He scooped Jackson into his arms, pressing his forehead against the crown of Jackson's hair. He held Jackson as closely as he could because it was going to be the last time.

"Alel? What's wrong? Did you fall asleep making dinner and have a bad dream?"

Fuck. Dinner.

"Dinner's ready." Alel cringed. "Go eat while I pack your things."

"Pack my things?" Jackson laughed, combing Alel's long hair. "Are we eloping? I think it's a little soon."

"We're going to church." Alel held his breath. His muscles tensed. Alel tried to keep in the tears, but they came to the brink of his eyes: too hot, hot as hellfire, and far, far too human. He should not be crying.

"Alel?" Jackson pulled back. He cupped Alel's face in his hands and brushed the tears away with his thumbs. "What's wrong? What happened?"

Alel sniffed and wiped at his nose. He pulled away so he could dry his face with his shirt and try to breathe enough to rein in some control over himself.

"Lust. Found me. I—I can't. I can fight an archangel, but the Sins are on par with the Principalities. I don't care what happens to me, but I want you to be safe!" Alel burst into another round of sobs. To escape his tears, he stood up, went to the kitchen, and sliced the lasagna into squares. He turned to fetch a plate, but Jackson stood behind him. Gently, Jackson grabbed the spatula out of Alel's hands, set it aside, and held Alel's shoulders while looking him in the eyes.

"I'm not hiding in a church for the rest of my life."

"And I'm not going to let you be raped and murdered."

Jackson's eyes rounded, huge and shocked.

"They're demons, Jackson." Alel hissed. His voice was cruel, but he *needed* Jackson to understand the truth. "Not me and Naberius. We've been living with humans for thousands of years. We've changed, but Lust—Lust *has no humanity*. They will make your death slow. They will do the *worst* possible things they can imagine."

"I—"

"We can't debate this. We're finding a church to take you in, and then I'm leaving."

"Leaving? Where are you going?" Jackson screamed.

"Far away from you!" Alel wrenched himself from Jackson's grip. "Eat. I'll pack a bag for you."

"Hell, no! This is some Ophelia bullshit and I'm not hiding in a monastery and never seeing you again!" Jackson paced the length of the kitchen. "There has to be *something* we can do. What about Sariel?"

"Sariel is the worst angel on the planet!"

"But can't she ask God? I mean, we live in a world with literal fucking angels and demons; that means God's real, right? Can't God help?"

"You can ask God for help if you want." Alel gave a helpless shrug. "I mean, I tried earlier and pissed Lust off. I didn't know what else to do. I guess we can both ask, but God usually doesn't *do* anything? At least not directly."

"This is shit! Total shit! Fuck!" Jackson slumped to the kitchen floor. He pulled his knees to his chest and pressed his hands together.

"I don't think you have to do the thing with the hands." Alel dropped in front of him, but he pressed his palms together as well.

He didn't know how to pray. Should he ramble? So many prayers seemed to be people whining for something, and Alel was the rule, not the exception. He only wanted Jackson safe. He begged to keep Jackson safe. They sat in tense silence, struggling with their thoughts, and then flung their arms around each other, both crying. Jackson's cheek burned against Alel's, and the tears made their skin itch, but he didn't want to pull away. A cool hand pressed on his cheek. Jackson's hands were warm, so Alel blinked away his tears and looked up. Sariel had a hand on each of them. She frowned.

"Alel, what's wrong? Jackson didn't call me, but I heard, no I *felt* a Voice, and it wanted me to check on you."

"Lust." Alel's voice cracked when he spoke.

"Oh...oh, I'm sorry. This is all my fault isn't it?" Sariel used her forearm to brush away a single tear from her own cheek. "You saved me and the archangel retaliated by going to the Sins."

Alel nodded his head.

"Okay. Well okay, then. I have no idea what we're going to do, but we'll do something, yeah?"

"You have to find somewhere safe for Jackson." Alel avoided looking at either of his companions by staring at the gleam on the kitchen floor.

"No, for both of us," Jackson insisted.

"I'm going to get Naberius. I-I don't know, safety in numbers, I guess? We'll think of something together." Sariel disappeared.

Alel sighed and flung himself backward. He sprawled on the kitchen floor in the shape of a snow angel and stared at the overhead light until bleary dark circles danced across the ceiling.

"I guess I should set the table for four."

"I'll help." Jackson rubbed his face and stood. Jackson brewed coffee, and Alel grabbed plates and flatware. While measuring coffee grounds into the filter, Jackson said, "We'll make this work."

"I want you to know I've never been so happy. You gave me an opportunity to be myself, and I loved the person I ended up being. I've never felt that way before—content. With me, with us, with life. I've never—"

They were kissing and tugging at each other's shirts. Alel didn't want to stop; he decided to never stop. They'd kiss forever. A knock at the door interrupted them and Jackson made a frustrated, desperate noise. He pulled away and walked toward the living room. Forever hadn't lasted nearly long enough. Alel sighed and scooped heaping servings of lasagna on the plates and arranged them around the table. Naberius stormed into the kitchen. He dug his nails into Alel's shoulders and shook him.

"This is why I told you not to use their names! I told you not to talk to the food! We're forbidden to fall in love or I would have kissed you myself, idiot! Dammit, Alel!"

"Naberius. Calm down. I was *dying* before. I was starving myself to death but not anymore. What does it matter if they hurt me now?" Alel grabbed Naberius's wrists. He was too strong for Naberius to muscle out of the hold.

"Dying is better than what Lust will do!"

"Then protect Jackson for me." A glimmer flashed across Alel's skin as he narrowed his eyes.

"Stop it, you two. We're going to protect everyone." Sariel said, her voice calm. She sat in front of a plate and smiled up at Jackson. "This smells delicious."

"Alel made it." Jackson gestured toward Alel.

"That's not food, Alel!" Naberius screamed, pointing to Jackson. "That's food. You should have seduced him and left!"

"Shove it up your ass, Naberius." Jackson hammered his fists on the table and dropped into his seat.

"Screaming isn't going to make you less afraid," Alel said as he went to the table and shoved a bite of lasagna into his mouth.

"Don't act brave," Naberius hissed as his tail flicked in agitation and his wings shifted, relaxing and folding again in restless reflex.

"I'm not. Believe me, I'm not being brave about this, but I refuse to regret my choices. You'd do the same for Sariel."

"Everything I ever did..." Naberius clenched his fork handle. "Was so this wouldn't ever happen to you."

"I know." Alel nodded.

"But it happened anyway."

"Yes. It happened anyway. Naberius, I'm happy."

"What about five thousand years from now when you're so insane from torture you can't even *remember his name*."

Alel slammed his fork down. "Then carve his name into my chest so I can at least look at it!"

"I didn't spoon-feed you orgies for thousands of years for you to die or worse!" Naberius's talons sank into the table and splintered the wood.

"You force-fed me gruel! Of course, when someone comes along and offers me homemade pizza, I'm going to eat it!"

"He's being literal, you know." Jackson interrupted them with a sad laugh. "We were at a party and I literally offered him pizza. I was even specific about it not being a euphemism. I thought he was a vampire, and I was going to let myself be food for no other reason than to avoid the sex everyone always wanted when I dated them."

"It was awkward later when we figured out the misunderstanding." A sad smile curled up Alel's lips. "But it doesn't matter. The kind of sex I enjoy isn't the kind incubi are supposed to have. We're supposed to fuck, but it's as cruel as forcing grease down a goose's throat to fatten them up for foie gras; even when it tasted good, it left me sick afterward." Alel clenched his teeth. "I'm happy now, and I'm not regretting any of my choices."

Silence hit the room, dead, heavy, and stifling. No one ate much, and it made Alel sad to see all his work get stabbed with forks instead of eaten, so he started to eat his own.

"I wish we were human," Sariel whispered. "Then none of this would be a problem. I could be a girl; you two could get married."

"We're not the problem, heaven and hell are." Naberius nibbled on a bite of food, sighed, as if he hated all existence, and started eating it.

Jackson stood up. "Alel, marry me."

"What?" Alel almost choked. He took a drink and watched Jackson drop to one knee. "Jackson, we can't."

"Why not?"

"Because, I mean, demons don't..." Alel stumbled for reasons but found only excuses. The idea had never occurred to him simply because he'd never heard of a demon getting married.

"Naberius can be the best man, and Sariel can be the maid of honor. We'll go elope. Right now. Let's do it. If they take you, they won't be stealing their demon—they'll be kidnapping my husband."

"That doesn't make a difference." Naberius shook his head.

"Who cares? It'll make a difference to us." He looked at Alel. "Right?"

Alel dropped to the floor so he could embrace Jackson. He laughed in Jackson's arms. They bumped noses and rocked side to side, and although hell would soon drag Alel into its depth, Alel forgot suffering existed as he rocked in Jackson's embrace.

"Fine. I'll drive." Naberius sighed.

"This is so exciting!" Sariel jumped to her feet. "I don't have anything to wear."

"We're eloping," Alel said. "The dress you're wearing now is perfect. None of us are changing our clothes."

"It's a shame, though. You two deserve a huge church wedding."

"A demon having a church wedding." Naberius snorted. "This is why Lust is going to rend his soul, and you guys are acting like this is a romcom."

"It's because I know I'm doomed that I want to suck the marrow from the bones." Alel stood and lifted Jackson into his arms. "Let's go get married."

Naberius drove, Sariel rode shotgun, and Alel and Jackson huddled together in the small back seat. They kept their fingers laced together the entire time. They stopped at the first jeweler for matching bands and then found the first chapel. Alel, Naberius, and Sariel had to wear their glamours, but Alel didn't pick his tall, dark, handsome stranger persona. He merely hid all his demonic attributes. He kept the freckles, however, changing them from lavender to brown, but leaving his skin speckled all over. Jackson smiled, tracing his fingers across the bridge of Alel's nose.

"You kept them for me?"

"I know you think they're cute." Alel held his breath, committing Jackson's touch to memory as best he could. He wanted to remember the current moment when the torture started; he wanted to hide in Jackson's touch even when hot iron pike screwed into his flesh and made him wail.

"It's the best wedding gift you could have thought to give me."

Alel nearly screamed every time they had to sign more paperwork. His eyes darted around the room full of flowers and last-minute odds and ends people might need to buy: ring pillows, bouquets, champagne glasses for toasting. They bought four glasses and a bottle of champagne so they could all toast afterward, and Alel bought a small bouquet. He didn't need it, but he thought Sariel would have fun catching it afterward.

The music was cliché; they hadn't had time to pick a song. The room resembled a cross between a funeral parlor and a fast food restaurant, but Alel ignored the ugly paisley carpet and kept his eyes on Jackson's face. Damn, he loved Jackson.

"I want to do our own vows," Jackson whispered to Alel when he stood beside them at the altar. Alel nodded, holding out his hand for Jackson to take. He slipped the ring on Alel's finger. "Neither heaven nor hell can change my love for you. They can chop the ring off your finger; they can torture you until you forget my name—your name now, too—but they can't take what we have. It's ours."

Tears slipped down Alel's cheeks. He was expecting something generic and gushy, but Jackson's vow showed he understand how dire the situation was.

"Neither heaven nor hell," Alel repeated as he put the second ring onto Jackson's fingers. They'd chosen titanium because they wanted something stronger than gold. "can change my love for you. Jackson, I wish I could say I won't forget you. I wish I could say I'll secretly love you even after ten thousand years, but I've seen what they do... I can't lie: I will forget your name; I will forget why this moment was worth it, but that will never change the fact that this moment *was worth it*, and forgetting your name will never change the fact that from this day on, I'll be Alel Banks."

If the reverend was confused, he didn't show it. Alel wondered if he was even listening, and he almost hoped he wasn't. The moment was for him and Jackson alone. The reverend went through the motions of pronouncing them spouses and nodded at Jackson.

"You may kiss your beloved."

Jackson grabbed Alel and dipped him. Alel gasped, breathless as their lips met. As soon as he was back on his feet, Sariel was grabbing him and sobbing happy tears into his T-shirt. They were shepherded into a small reception area as grand as a walk-in closet, but it gave them a private spot to open the champagne and clink their glasses together without the bother of their glamours. They downed the drinks, the inevitable gnawing at their nerves despite their joy.

Naberius grabbed Alel by the shoulders and kissed him. Alel relaxed and blushed, tasting strawberries. He remembered all their nights together, how strawberries often found their way into the meal somehow. He'd never known Naberius was the one to add them to the dish. They kissed once more. It was something they should have done thousands of years ago, and it needed to be done, even if it was a goodbye kiss.

"I'm sorry," Naberius whispered when he broke the kiss. "I'm so selfish. I wanted you alive more than happy. I always told myself unhappy and underfed were better for you than the punishment for infernal treason."

"I'm grateful." Alel wrapped his arms around Naberius's waist and grinned against his chest. "I understood you were doing your best."

"I hope this helps, somehow, when it's all too late." Naberius shook his head. His eyes were glassy. "I hope this moment spares you for at least a hundred years."

"I'm so happy for you both, and I'm not worried, not one bit. I have faith you'll be okay." Sariel stole Alel from Naberius's arms and also kissed his mouth, although hers was a fleeting, congratulatory kiss.

"Oh great, *now* you want to be an angel and have faith in love."

"I may be a terrible angel, but I have always had faith in love." Sariel gave Alel's chest a mock punch. She grabbed Jackson and gave his lips a brief kiss as well, cupping his cheek and smiling. "You're the best human I've ever watched over, and I'm glad I'm your friend as well as your guardian angel."

"I'm glad I got the rebellious angel who's as much of a misfit as I am." Jackson smiled at her. Then he gave Naberius a hug. "Take care of my angel for eternity. Don't think I won't sneak out of heaven after I die to kick your ass if you treat her badly."

"Jackson, be better to Alel than I was."

"Don't worry, I'm a much better cook than you." Jackson smirked at his own double entendre. Then Jackson took Alel's hands, and Alel lost his breath again.

"Is it time for the honeymoon?" Alel kissed Jackson's forehead.

"Yes." Jackson pulled Alel into his chest, kissing the side of his face. Alel turned his head, and their lips brushed together.

Alel thought back to when he was terrified of kissing, when he feared hell enough to behave. His entire life until Jackson had been as lonely as waiting for a train in an empty station. When Jackson pulled Alel back to his feet, Alel wrapped his wings around them both and coiled his tail around Jackson's waist. They kissed again, and again, and again. They couldn't breathe, and they were happily gasping for air between each pass.

"I love you," Alel whispered, too out of breath to say it louder.

"I love you." Jackson curled his arms around Alel's neck and pulled them together for yet another kiss.

Chapter Twelve

THE GLOW OF the moment clung to them, bright and crackling with energy. They held each other and kneaded their lips together, but a sudden screech tearing through the air broke their kisses. The air boiled around them, a shimmering mirage. Sweat broke out on their faces and rolled down their backs. Despite the heat, Alel clung to Jackson.

"We're out of time," Alel said.

"No." Jackson's iris darted from left to right as he scanned the room.

Shadows surrounded them. They rolled and churned, black waves cresting and crashing around them. Shapes formed and disappeared. Alel counted two dozen demons. He was proud of the number despite his terror. He must have hurt Lust a fair amount if they brought such a large guard to collect him.

"Jackson, you should run." Alel released Jackson, but Jackson shook his head.

"I'm not letting go." Jackson's fingers dug into the fabric of Alel's shirt.

Sariel dropped to her knees and chanted, repeating the Our Father in a continuous loop. A soft glow surrounded her, and Alel pulled Jackson closer to her aura.

"*Our Father who art in heaven, hallowed be Thy name...*"

"Don't." Jackson choked on the emotion in his voice. His nails pierced Alel's biceps.

"I love you." Alel kissed Jackson.

"Thy kingdom come. Thy will be done..."

"Don't, please, Alel, don't—"

"Pray." Alel gave Jackson's forehead a final kiss and pressed him to his knees.

Sariel circled her wings around him like a force field. She took his hands, never pausing or stuttering in her continuous chant. Jackson looked shell-shocked. The shadows in the room grew and the shapes became more distinct. He started muttering with Sariel. He missed words and fumbled the parts he knew, but he kept rambling even as tears ran down his face.

"I don't see why you're all so worked up." Naberius used his tail to swipe the champagne flutes and bottle off the small table. He hopped on it, lifting up his tail from between his legs and nibbling on it in mock, nervous seduction. "Those angels were mad because I was fucking one of their own. Alel got rid of them. We should be getting *rewarded*, not harassed. Why don't you peons go scurry home and explain that to Lust?"

"It's okay, Naberius." Alel stared at Jackson. "We knew this was unavoidable. You don't have to defend me."

"Shut the fuck up, Alel. If I want you to talk, I'll shove my cock up your ass and make you scream blasphemies. Otherwise stand there and look pretty. It's what you're good at." He addressed the shadowed forms. "Alel has seduced more virgins than any other incubus or succubus I know. So what if he's playing a slow game with this one? He was just waiting to consummate the marriage, then he was going to leave the kid and break his heart. You dumb fucks ruined all that pain and suffering by showing up uninvited."

"How sweet." Lust's voice rang from the air. The Sin materialized behind Naberius, stroking his wings and making him blush and squirm the moment they touched him. "You're trying to protect your ex-lover. You two have always been close, haven't you?"

"Shit," Naberius cursed as the Sin toyed with Naberius's claws at the tips of his wings. "That...bastard made me fat by hand-feeding me virgins... *Shit, ah, fuck!* Why-why wouldn't I stick around?"

"Do you love him?" The Sin bit the ridge of Naberius's wing, enticing him to be honest.

"*Ahh!*"

"Answer." They bit again.

"I don't know!" He whined as he clutched the table with his claws.

"What about the little angel?" Lust licked up the ridge and then back down.

"I'm *fucking* the angel!" Naberius growled.

"I want the truth." Lust bit Naberius's wing for a third time.

"I don't fucking know how to tell the truth! I'm one of yours, you crazy dumb cunt!"

"You truly are." Lust laughed and ruffled the hair between Naberius's horns. "And it's simple enough to prove you have no loyalty to them. Go kill the angel for me. Its chanting is giving me a headache."

"You want *me*. These others? They're useless. Take me and let's go." Alel rushed to the table where Lust and Naberius sat. He rested his hands on Naberius's thighs, leaning around Naberius so he could stare directly at Lust.

"Kill the angel, Naberius, and I'll reward you personally." Lust spread their fingers out against the scales of Naberius's wings. Naberius grunted in ecstasy.

His breath came out in harsh puffs, and his eyes were glassy and lost. Alel's mind raced for a way to distract Lust from the others. He shoved Naberius to the floor. The demon groaned, worked up and sensitive from Lust's ministrations. Alel threaded his fingers through the Sin's hair and pulled their faces close.

"I'm jealous," he snarled. It was as if all his pretty lying skills came back to him in a flash. "Don't pet him. Pet me."

"You?" Lust snorted. "You've been bad."

"Then punish me."

"I know this is a feint. Spreading your legs won't save your precious friends and lovers."

"So I'm completely faking?" Alel asked. The strongest Sin wasn't Lust—it was Pride—and the most beautiful lies were almost completely honest. "If you admit I have no interest in you, then it means your powers don't work against me. Did you create a failure?" Alel grinned. "Is love stronger than you, Lust? Are you saying you can't tame me? What will the other Sins think of you? Couldn't even manage a little incubus because he got a boyfriend. What a shame—"

The Sin slapped him; the blow torqued his head to the left. A trickle of blood rolled down Alel's bottom, split lip, but he only dabbed his tongue at it and smiled at Lust.

"You know the second we leave, my guards are tearing them to shreds, don't you?"

"Is this the part where I give a heroic love-conquers-all speech?" Alel's breath washed over Lust's lips. "Or are you going to take me home so we can skip the clichés?"

Deep inside he yearned for a miracle he knew wouldn't come. However, there'd been a time when Alel yearned to be kissed, and not only did he discover the joy, the thrill, and the euphoria of kissing since then, but he'd fallen in love, so Alel thought hoping for a miracle wasn't the most foolish thing he'd ever done in his existence.

WHEN ALEL WENT up to Lust, Jackson tensed. He prepared to jump up, to scream, to run toward his husband and die protecting him only for his ghost to spring from his body and continue right where he'd left off. But as Sariel prayed and Jackson muttered half-formed words. A hand touched Jackson's shoulder. He knew no one stood behind him. Sariel knelt in front of him, Alel and Naberius sat at the table with Lust, and the demons stayed in the shadows while waiting for directions. Still, Jackson felt the touch, and with it, calm washed over him. His prayer didn't improve, each word tumbled out of his mouth without grace or clarity, but Jackson knew it was okay. He stayed with Sariel. He tried to mimic her prayer, but the moment Alel disappeared, Jackson jumped to his feet.

"Alel!"

The shadows hissed. Their forms were visible now. Their horns rose into the air taller than spears. Barbs poked from their tails, sharp enough to lash chunks of flesh away with each strike. The edges of their serrated claws were as sharp as obsidian. Jackson stood in place, balling his fists. He wondered if he could land at least one punch before they turned him to a heap of gore.

He never found out. Sariel jumped in front of him while clutching a flaming sword.

"Naberius, guard Jackson!" She shouted.

Naberius crawled on hands and knees. He grabbed Jackson by the hand and yanked him to a crouch so he could tortoise shell over him. Meanwhile, Sariel charged the nearest demon. The flaming blade sliced through the demons as if they were soot. They crumbled and faded back into shadows as she fought. Jackson couldn't see well through the barrier of Naberius's body and wings, but each glimpse he caught made him gasp. Streaks of yellow and orange followed each stroke, leaving smeary afterimages in Sariel's path.

And there she was, in black heels, in scarlet lipstick, in a black, spaghetti-strap dress dappled with glittery silver skulls, and Jackson couldn't ask for a better guardian angel. She decimated the demons and then sheathed the sword in a scabbard at her hip. She walked toward them, stopping in front of them both and extending her hand.

"How?" Naberius asked, still crouching over Jackson as if to protect him from Sariel as well. "You—you shouldn't even have a sword. And a flaming one? Not even the archangels have flaming swords."

"It appeared...so I used it," she answered.

Naberius closed his eyes, held his breath, and reached out his hand. She took it and pulled him to his feet. They stared at each other a moment. He gave her a shy smile.

"I'm so hard up right now."

Sariel started laughing.

"I can't help it!"

"I know! It's okay! Lust was tormenting you. I'm sorry, Naberius. I'll make it up to you later." She glanced at Jackson, who was already standing. "Jackson, I know you're brave—"

"We're going, right?" he interrupted her, "You're going to take me to hell, and we're going to get Alel back."

"Jackson, we can't—" Naberius broke in, but Sariel cut him off.

"Yes. That's exactly what we're going to do."

"Sariel, your sword is impressive, but maybe not marching-into-the-depths-of-hell-and-challenging-one-of-the-Sins impressive."

"You don't think so?" Sariel asked. "Then pull it from the scabbard."

"Um, it looks pretty holy. Not exactly a toy I can play with."

"Naberius, I prayed. This sword appeared. Alel made me his guardian angel. I'm going to do my job."

"Thank you, Sariel." Jackson threw his arms around her.

"Jackson, you have to hold my hand the entire time. Don't let go."

"I won't." Jackson nodded as he pulled away.

"Naberius? I need you to show me the way."

"No." He stepped back, shaking his head, sweating in fear. "No fucking way. I'm not leading you two to your deaths. I'm not losing you too!"

"Naberius."

"Alel wouldn't forgive me if I took Jackson there!"

"I'll find another guide if I have to," Sariel threatened. "I'd rather have someone I trusted."

"Fuck," Naberius swore, his tail whipping about in a frenzy, and his folded wings twitched. "Fuck! Fine!"

He grabbed Jackson by the wrist and pulled him close. It surprised Jackson, and he tried to pull away, but Naberius held him tightly. He raised his tail and darted it forward; the barb pierced Jackson's palm and he hissed at the unexpected pain. Naberius flicked Jackson's hand in a wide arc, dotting the floor with red specks.

"What the fuck?" Jackson finally managed to pull his hand away and press it against his shirt to try to slow the bleeding.

"I needed innocent blood."

"Could have *warned* me."

"No, the fear is part of the spell." Naberius clenched his teeth. "Everything about being a demon is vile. You should understand that because we're going home."

He muttered something Jackson didn't catch, but it made his skin crawl and his stomach churn. A black door appeared in front of them. It stood in the middle of the reception room.

"I didn't expect something so...ordinary," Jackson said.

"Don't let appearances fool you." Naberius opened it.

Jackson expected a smell—a thick stench of sulfur and burnt flesh—but there was nothing. Nothing. No sound, no smell, no light; it was a deprivation chamber.

"I hate this place," Naberius whispered. "Haven't been back since I came here."

"Fear not." Sariel pulled out her sword. The flames revealed a very normal-looking hallway. It fit perfectly with the rest of the wedding chapel.

"This can't be—"

"It is." Naberius interrupted Jackson again. "I'm not sure how it actually looks. This is probably a lie. Or maybe it isn't. It's always too hard to tell what's real."

The hallway had yellow wallpaper, old and cozy. It was someone's grandmother's hallway. There'd be a door at the end with a bathroom with a padded toilet seat and a doll with a crocheted dress hiding the extra toilet paper and a cameo picture hanging on the wall next to the door. It *couldn't* be hell. Jackson couldn't believe it, but when he glanced at Naberius, he noticed the demon trembled.

"Hold my hand," Sariel reminded. Jackson took her free hand, the other held out the sword, using it as a torch. "You too, Naberius, hold onto me."

"But—"

"Naberius, don't you dare let go of me once you hold on."

He gave her a little growl but wrapped his tail around her waist. Jackson held his breath until it cramped his chest, and then he blew it out. They walked forward, and with a few more steps, they were on hideous shag carpet. Pictures hung in rows along the walls. Jackson's eyes wandered to the old black-and-white photos. He'd been so fooled by the harmless, '70s, homey aesthetic, he expected some ancient family portrait to be hanging on the wall, but it wasn't.

It was a photograph of Alel, beaten and decapitated, his blood pooling like ink around his corpse. Jackson winced, squeezing Sariel's hand until his own hurt.

"Don't look," Naberius shut his own eyes.

"I won't." Jackson focused on the sword.

The flames near the blade glimmered violet and indigo, which softened to yellow and white fire. Sariel kept a calm, steady face. It reminded Jackson of when the invisible hand touched his shoulder. He wondered if she experienced the same, and if perhaps that hand had given her the sword. Invisible claws scraped Jackson's calves. He gasped as hot ribbons of his own blood rolled down his skin and stuck to his jeans.

"It's not real," Sariel said. "I know it hurts, regardless."

"You too?" Jackson asked.

"Yes, I feel it too," she answered.

"So do I. It's our welcome."

"H-how bad does it get?" Jackson asked, flinching as needles pierced his skin.

His grip on Sariel's hand shook, the sweat from both their bodies making Jackson's hold slick, but he clutched to her because he somehow knew if he let go, the single hallway would become a maze and he'd be lost in it.

"Bad," Naberius said.

"So Alel went through this?" Jackson's jaw clenched, the pain adding to his anger.

"Worse, Jackson. It would have been worse. Lust was pissed at him."

"Then… I don't care…how much—*fuck*!" Nails rose up from the floor, impaling through the soles of their shoes into their feet. "I don't care how much it hurts!" Jackson shrieked, as if defying the pain could end it. Rats chittered behind the walls. Far away, the sounds of metal grinding raised the hairs on Jackson's neck. A sheet of glass cut him in half, but he forced one foot in front of the other, ignoring the trail of blood spreading behind him.

"It's not real," Sariel repeated.

Jackson nodded, his thumb slipped to his ring finger. The cool metal calmed his nerves despite the tears burning on his cheeks. Jackson figured if vampires and werewolves, demons and angels, God and hell were all real, then magic had to be real as well. Didn't it? And if magic was real, then a wedding ring in a cursed place would help him get through the pain. Thus, Jackson forced his feet forward, step after step, over nails, broken glass, flaming coals. Imaginary screws tightened into his tendons, but he gritted his teeth, hissed, and moved forward. Barbed wire wrapped around his throat. The barbs dug in, but the pain was nothing compared to the sudden tug stealing his breath. Jackson scratched at the wire spiraled around his neck. The barbs pierced his fingers and blood splattered to the floor in front of him, but he didn't care. He choked, mind screaming for air. Laughter ricocheted around him as the barbs burst into flame and evaporated. He doubled over, gasping.

"I've got you," Sariel's voice pushed through the frantic fog in Jackson's mind.

She lifted him into her arms and carried him. Jackson cried against Sariel's shoulder. A lash tore his back to ribbons. Stripe after stripe after stripe, and each lash cut deeper than the previous. He couldn't… He couldn't… He thought he'd be strong enough to endure anything, face any challenge. Jackson screamed. Wasn't love supposed to *beat* evil? He wailed as something gnawed off his fingers. Even in hell, Jackson couldn't doubt his love. It was real, but it couldn't save him from the needles twisting into every single nerve of his body. The tears rushed over his cheeks. He screamed.

NABERIUS WAS IMPRESSED by how long Jackson lasted, but in the end, he'd collapsed. Every human to ever walk through the abyss broke at some point. Sariel cradled him in her arms, the sword tilting to an awkward angle as she balanced both the blade and Jackson.

"I could carry him," Naberius offered, his tail still wrapped around her waist.

"No, I have to protect him."

"You can't use a sword with a human in your arms."

"Then take the sword, not the human."

"You know I won't. It turned demons stronger than me to ash."

"Even at the end, even with Lust standing in front of you, you *still* tried to help Alel. Are you telling me a few flames are too much for you?"

"Yes."

"You're a coward, Naberius."

"Always have been." Naberius snorted and the sorrow in his chest was bitter. "Alel was the brave one, calling people by their names, touching them, treating them better than a quick fuck. I never had the guts."

"This is a good chance for redemption, don't you think?"

"No, I think it's a good chance to throw our lives away."

"Naberius, I can do this alone, but we're stronger together," Sariel said.

"Stronger than what?"

"Let's find out. Help me. Take my sword."

Even in hell, she glowed. Naberius thought of how bright Sariel was without her clothing, sheer white fire, much worse than the sword.

"Gimme." He clasped the blade.

It burned his hand, blistering the pads of his palm and wrist, but he held it out so Sariel could see. Naberius extended his left wing and wrapped it around her, as if he could protect her from the endless cuts and torments he knew she felt. Of course he couldn't, he couldn't even hold the sword without hurting himself. What right did he have to dare to love an angel?

But he did, and he proved it the moment the first demon appeared—a succubus, low level, a pawn no better than himself. She sauntered toward him, confident. She licked her lips and pinched his nipple through the fabric of his shirt. Naberius plunged the sword through her stomach. Her face froze, shocked, her eyes glazed like morning frost creeping across a window pane, and she crumbled to ash. The stroke had been clumsy; Naberius hadn't used a sword in over a hundred years, but the flames consumed her whole. Killing his own was a final act of treason, one he couldn't excuse.

And the damnedest part was it made Naberius happy. They'd both be exiles, but he couldn't imagine anyone fiercer he'd rather be exiled with for the rest of eternity.

"You didn't have to," Sariel said. She understood the weight of what he'd done.

"Yeah, I did. Let's keep walking. I'm not great with the thing, but I'll make sure nothing touches either one of you."

"How much farther?" Sariel asked.

"Forever. Eternity." Naberius shook his head. "Don't think about how long. It will drive you mad."

Several spirits of rage surrounded them. Steam drifted from the man-shaped lumps of cooling magma. Naberius bit the inside of his cheek.

"Sariel, I have to let go. I need to fight them."

"Come back to me when you're done," Sariel whispered as she pressed her back against the wall to avoid the battle.

The soft longing in her voice made him smile. He remembered the fumbling, desperate, lust-crazed angel who couldn't keep their hands off Naberius months and months ago. He wondered when their curiosity and desire had turned into this? Them versus hell. Naberius spun the sword in warning; the flames danced. The old cell memory of training came back to him like a dream often would, little hints and large fragments. Naberius pushed forward. The more strokes he made, the more he remembered, until he stood alone with the sword burning both his hands. Naberius grunted. The pain of a thousand swords pierced him at once although nothing was there. Sariel stood pressed against the wall, her face twisted in agony. He ran to her, cupping her cheek.

"I'm...okay." She smiled a fake smile. "It's only pain. We have to keep moving, right?"

"That's right," he whispered, forcing himself forward. He smelled burning flesh while his skin crackled and charred.

"Promise me..." Sariel gasped. "Promise me we'll get there. No matter what."

"Yes." If it came to it, he wasn't sure if he could carry Sariel and Jackson both. He swore to himself he would, but the sword shook in Naberius's hand. He didn't know how they were going to reach Lust's chambers.

Chapter Thirteen

ALEL BLINKED TO clear the tears in his eyes. They itched as they stained his cheeks and throat. Lust's hands were soft. They'd chosen a feminine form with which to torment Alel. She nibbled up his neck and along his jaw. Alel shut his eyes and turned away, wondering if Jackson was somehow okay. Was he somehow okay? Was he somehow okay? Lust's palm pressed against Alel's crotch and she growled.

"Why aren't you hard?" Alel opened his bleary, tear-glazed eyes and gave her an incredulous look. She frowned at him, lips perfect and red, but Alel had no desire to kiss them. Lust was empty; there'd be no *substance* behind her kisses. She straddled him. Her inner thighs were warm through his clothes. The strap of her dress fell over the creamy skin of her shoulder. It was lovely. Alel understood that it was lovely the way one understood a painting, but it stirred nothing within him, especially with not knowing if Jackson was dead or alive. He closed his eyes and begged for Jackson to be alive. The sting of Lust's palm against his cheek brought him back to the moment.

"Stop praying!" she screamed.

"Was I?" he asked. "I was never sure how to."

"Liar."

A bitter sound pushed past his throat. He always had been quite the liar, but he'd gotten more and more accustomed to the truth each time he told Jackson he loved him.

"I know what you want." Lust slipped her fingers through Alel's long hair and drew their faces closer together. "You desire forbidden fruit, don't you?"

She leaned close, parting her lips. Alel flinched and turned his head to avoid her mouth. Another slap clipped his cheek. Her nails caught his skin, and a warm trickle ran down his cheekbone, but to Alel it was just another tear, and he didn't care. She sneered at him, hissing, but then a smug look brightened her face.

"How about this?" she asked, and then she changed.

The softer features of their face grew broader, so did their chest and arms. Their body weight grew heavier against Alel's body, hands coarse, hair short, and their floral perfume shifted to an oak-heavy cologne. He was nice to admire. Someone Alel would have enjoyed watching on a movie screen, but not Jackson. Not his Jackson. Not his husband.

Lust leaned in, kissing Alel again. It was worse, somehow, with him as a man, because part of Alel knew he *should* have coveted it. Lust was a handsome, higher level demon, and Alel was an incubus. It should have been a power trip to be kissed by him. His body should yield wholly to the personification of lust, but Alel's face twisted in discomfort. His whole body trembled, but not with desire. It was a strange, hideous sensation. Alel's nerves lit up, but with the wrong sort of light, the piss-yellow light of a low-income-apartment hallway, not sunlight, not the sunlight that slipped into Jackson's apartment the morning when they first kissed. Alel remembered the way the sunlight lit Jackson's hair, a shining halo, something divine.

"Stop!" Lust growled. "You taste disgusting. Stop it!"

"I hope you choke on it." Alel gritted teeth and held his breath for a punch that never came. Instead, Lust was smoothing his fingers through Alel's hair. The delicate caresses were worse than the slaps.

"Shhhh, shhhhh, I'm not going to hurt you. Relax."

"Fling me into a bed of coals. Impale me on a sharpened stick. Do anything that isn't this."

"I'm not sure how you became this broken, but I'll fix you, and when I'm done, you'll *beg* to go back to earth to fuck." Lust laughed. "Then we'll have fun with the bed of coals."

"I'm not broken." Alel shook his head.

"Of course you are." He brushed his bottom lip along the shell of Alel's ear. "But first you need to admit it."

Alel hated how much demons lied...how much he used to lie to try to fit in. Alel lay down, so Lust had full access to his body. He stared at the ceiling, refusing to think about anything. He thought about the ceiling.

"You're going to have to take what you want," Alel said.

"Not yet; you're not aroused. Why aren't you aroused? Naberius reacted properly."

"Everything you do hurts my stomach."

"You're mine," he hissed. "You were made to *want* this."

"I want to hold Jackson."

"You're mine." He grabbed Alel's hair and yanked his head, bringing their faces together.

Alel studied Lust's face. His lips were twisted into an angry sneer, and the rage made his features ugly.

"It truly bothers you, doesn't it? Not having power over someone." Alel sighed. "All my life I slept with people because I thought I'd starve without it, and I enjoy sex, so it didn't seem to be a problem, but..." Alel closed his eyes. He didn't want to see Lust anymore. "Now I know better. I don't love you. I don't want sex with you, so take what you want or flay me in punishment, either way..." His sobs were gentle, but his shoulders shook.

"Fine." Lust flipped Alel onto his stomach and shoved Alel's face into the mattress. "Then I will take what I want from you. Over and over until you *beg for it*."

Alel held his breath and squeezed his eyes shut until his head hurt. His breathing grew shallow, near hyperventilating, but even if his mouth wasn't pressed into silk sheets, he didn't think he'd be able to catch his breath.

"And stop praying!" Lust smacked the side of Alel's head, making it throb.

He could barely think, so Alel didn't know how he could be praying. He tried to blank his mind out, ignoring how Lust ripped through Alel's shirt with his claws and bit his shoulder. He told himself to relax. It was going to hurt, but if he relaxed, it'd hurt less, but it was impossible to relax when he *did not want this to be happening.*

A wet, gurgling sound from above made Alel jerk. He expected a lick against his exposed skin, but warm drops rained onto his back instead. Alel blinked his eyes open, staring at the silk sheets below him. The teardrop splatters became a rush of liquid fire pouring over his back. Alel coughed from the smell of sulfur, and a dead weight crushed him against the mattress.

"Don't you...fucking touch...my husband." Jackson's voice was weak and gasping for air, but real and distinctly *Jackson's* voice.

Alel twisted around so he could see what was happening. Lust's weight pinned him, but Jackson pushed Lust to the side. Blood steamed as it dribbled down the Sin's chin. The tip of a flaming sword protruded from Lust's chest, the pommel jutted out his back. It wasn't enough to kill Lust—one couldn't kill a Sin—but it bound him, and he couldn't move.

And Jackson *was* there. Pale, fevered, sweat-stained, and exhausted, but *there*—with Sariel and Naberius behind him. They rolled Lust onto the floor, and Jackson scooped Alel into his arms.

"I'm sorry." Jackson's voice sounded husky. He buried his face in Alel's hair and whispered again. "I'm sorry."

"No no, don't be sorry." Alel shook his head. He reached up and tangled his fingers into Jackson's hair. The stench of demon blood burned in their nostrils, but they refused to let go of each other. "You're alive; you're alive! How did you escape?"

"Sariel fought them off."

Alel's gaze flicked to the floor and the sword keeping Lust paralyzed. At the same moment, Sariel knelt beside Lust. She still wore her little black dress with glittery skulls, but her mascara left inky trails on her cheeks from the sweat and tears of her journey. As if aware, Sariel wiped her face before staring at the demon.

"I know you can hear me, so you'd better listen to what I'm saying. I don't give a single fuck if you're one of the most powerful demons in all of hell. Alel doesn't belong to you anymore; do you understand me? He married the human, and their bond was sealed by God. You interfere with their lives again, and next time, it won't be a human with a borrowed sword who attacks you. Next time, it will be me, and I've already been banished from heaven, so there's nothing keeping me from being merciless toward you."

As if to prove her point, Sariel twisted the sword and made Lust scream in agony. With another turn, she ripped the blade from Lust's back. The demon opened his mouth to speak, but couldn't manage more than a gasp. Sariel dangled her sword above Lust's throat.

"If you're smart, you'll let this go and never mention it. You don't want the other Sins to find out you were defeated in battle by a mere human, right? Or that one of your demons gave up tempting mortals because he fell in love? You'd be the center of infernal scandal."

Sariel sheathed her sword. Blood gushed from the wound in Lust's chest. Lust stayed on the floor, gasping for breath and pressing a hand against his body to stop the streaming blood.

"Humans...die." Lust gasped, glaring at Alel with the full hatred of a demon. "And then you'll be alone."

"No." Alel smiled, wrapped up in Jackson's arms. "Then I'll break into heaven and find him the same way he found me here. I've already sworn it."

"Come on." Jackson lifted Alel into his arms. He still looked half dead from his journey through hell but held on to Alel as if the universe might unravel otherwise. "I'm taking you home."

"This is real, right?" Alel shook. "It's not a lie hell made up to ruin me?"

"You tell me." Jackson bent his head and dragged his bottom lip against Alel's top one.

It was too tender, too sweet, too deliberate to be an illusion created by hell. Alel moaned; he relaxed into Jackson's arms. His shaking eased, and his skin glowed with all the affection he felt for Jackson.

"Okay, you two." Naberius pulled a face. "Wait until you're back home before you start your honeymoon."

"You can't...possibly...glow so brightly." Lust wept as the Sin curled onto his side and shielded his eyes with an outreached hand. "Only angels glow so bright."

"I told you," Sariel said. "Alel doesn't belong to you anymore."

"Go," the Sin snarled, teeth bared, tears of pain streaming down his face, although the hole in his chest was already smaller than it'd been moments ago. "You vile, *loathsome* filth. You're banished. All of you! Never, *ever*, return!"

A second later, they reappeared in the wedding chapel's reception room as if nothing had happened. The switch was so quick Jackson stumbled as if experiencing vertigo. He set Alel down, and they held onto each other for support.

"This is better than the time we got kicked out of Denny's for fucking the entire staff in the break room." Naberius swished his tail at the memory. "Remember that, Alel?"

"I don't know how I ever let you talk me into half the stuff we did." Alel laughed.

"Do you realize I've been officially exiled from *both* heaven and hell? I'm kinda proud of myself." Sariel grinned.

"Stupid angel, pride's a sin," Alel whispered. He teased her out of old habit, but his attention was on Jackson. Alel couldn't pull his gaze away from Jackson, who stared back with equal ferocity.

"Well, I can't go to hell for it, so I'm not at all concerned." She smacked Naberius's ass. "Go buy more champagne. I think we need another toast."

"I'm not your dog," Naberius complained, even as he left to go do as Sariel asked.

"Are you really all right?" Jackson smoothed his fingers up Alel's high cheekbones.

"I'm perfect." Alel held Jackson's face in return. "I was rescued from hell by my true love. It's hard to find that quality of romance in a fairytale, let alone real life."

"I passed out. The pain was too much, Sariel had to carry me for most of the trip." Jackson shook his head, tears in his eyes. "I revived right before we found Lust's chambers. I wasn't sure how I was going to help, but…when I saw that bastard on top of you—" Jackson's voice choked. "I-I didn't even realize I took the sword from Sariel's hands until I could smell the blood."

"I swear, I'm okay." Alel raised up on his toes and kissed Jackson's forehead. "So don't cry."

Jackson nodded and wiped his face. Naberius appeared with a cold, sweating bottle of unopened champagne, and Sariel found their glasses on the floor from earlier.

"Let's try this again. This time without the kidnapping and epic quest." Naberius popped the cork. Foam rushed down the sides and dripped to the carpet as he poured the drink into their glasses.

Alel dropped to a steel folding chair. He meant to sip the drink, but his nerves were quaking from the day's experiences, and he downed the glass in one shot. Jackson sat beside him, and by the way he chugged his own drink, Alel knew he felt the same.

"Guess if we can go through all this on day one, then there isn't anything life could throw at us our marriage couldn't handle."

"True." Alel smiled, winding his tail around Jackson's waist and pulling their bodies closer together.

"Let's get the kids home." Naberius nudged Sariel with his elbow. "So we can go back to my place for adult time."

"Your one-track mind is your most endearing quality." Sariel pushed him back as if he stood too close, but he wrapped them up in his wings and squeezed their bodies together.

"Or we could do it right here. I don't mind."

"Let's take Jackson and Alel home first." Sariel winked. "It's fun to watch you squirm."

They kept the glasses they'd bought as souvenirs and crowded back into Naberius's car. Sariel spent the entire ride playing coy as she spoke in innuendos as if she was too innocent to know how Naberius would take her words. Alel smiled at them from the back seat but only half-paid attention to their banter. Jackson was asleep against Alel's shoulder, and Alel kept thanking God over and over again the moment was real and not an illusion. When the car stopped in front of Jackson's apartment, Sariel got out and went to help Alel carry Jackson upstairs.

"It's okay." Alel shook his head as he cradled Jackson in his arms. "I want to do it. Humans carry their spouses across the threshold of their home, right?"

"No one really does that anymore." Sariel laughed as she reached out and held Alel's shoulder. "I don't think Lust will come after you again. At this point they'd save more face letting us all go than wasting more time and resources to hunt us, but if you need me—"

"Thanks, Sariel, but we're good." Alel's face softened. "Seriously, thank you. You saved Jackson. I can't repay you—"

"I'm so glad we're friends!" Sariel wrapped her arms around Alel. Her hold was awkward, with Jackson in his arms, but she made it work. "I was lonely too. That's why I used to pester you so much. I knew you'd put up with me, but now I know how delicious potato chips are, and sex, and..." She sniffed, using a fist to rub at her eyes while her other arm continued to hold onto Alel. "How about you sweet-talk Jackson in making pizza next Saturday, and then we can all go bowling afterward."

"Sounds fun." Alel grinned. He glanced at Naberius behind the wheel of his car. The other incubus stuck a finger down his throat, pretending to gag at the emotional scene, but Alel could tell he was also happy. He turned back to Sariel. "Haven't you tormented Naberius long enough?"

"Well, he did help save you too. I suppose I should reward him." She winked, kissed Alel's cheek, and then went back to the car. "Congratulations!"

Alel maneuvered Jackson up the stairs, across the threshold, and to their bedroom. He settled Jackson onto the mattress, pulled the covers over him, and slipped in next to him. Alel lay on his side so he could hold Jackson and rest his head on Jackson's chest. He covered them with one outstretched wing and wound his tail around Jackson's calf. Jackson's chest rose and fell, but Alel couldn't sleep. His mind raced. Jackson was in his arms. Jackson was alive. Jackson was his husband. He never had to worry about looking over his shoulder at shadows again. He could *live*.

He kept thinking until late morning sun softened the room with warm, buttercream tones. Jackson cooed and nuzzled under his chin.

"Where are we?"

"Home."

"Already?" Jackson sat up, examining the room. "We were in the car a second ago."

"That was yesterday." Alel sat up as well and leaned forward to kiss Jackson's cheek.

"Yesterday?" he shouted and Alel nodded. Jackson shook his head. "Alel, why didn't you wake me? It was our wedding night. I wanted to be with you."

"You were," Alel said. "We've been here together the entire time."

"No, I mean good, but...it was our *wedding night*." He drew imaginary pictures on the comforter. "I was going to do anything you asked me to."

"Well, in that case—" Alel grinned as he pulled Jackson back to their haven of blankets and pillows. "Let's stay in bed a little longer and keep doing exactly what we've been doing." He brushed his nose along the curve of Jackson's cheek. "Because this is exactly what I wanted."

"Okay." Jackson giggled. "Think the lasagna is still any good? I'm hungry for it now."

"I tossed it in the fridge before we eloped. It should be fine."

"Feed me lasagna breakfast in bed, then." Jackson chuckled.

"Okay." Alel sat back up.

"Wait." Jackson reached out for him.

"Yeah?" Alel stopped, turned, smiled at Jackson, and then settled beside him once again.

"We can do it tonight. However you want. Tell me how you want to make love…" Jackson blushed. "*Anything* okay? Don't hold back asking for something because you think I won't enjoy it."

"Actually…" Alel's tail wagged back and forth. Being married didn't make it less embarrassing when his tail decided to go off on its own. "There is something I-I think I've always wanted to do with someone but never had the courage to ask."

"Oh, okay." Jackson's face was a mix of nerves and curiosity. "What is it?"

Chapter Fourteen

SARIEL SLAMMED NABERIUS against the wall the moment they stepped inside his apartment. She dug her nails into the folds of his wings, making him squirm and call out, delirious and too into it to worry about how needy he sounded. And he *was* needy.

"Strip," Sariel ordered, but before he could, she yanked him by the hair and dragged him toward the bedroom.

She shoved him on the bed and wandered off to the bathroom sink to wash away the mascara smeared around her eyes. Naberius struggled out of his clothes. His tail slipped out of his pants easy enough, but his wings tangled in his shirt, and he swore and growled, fighting like a bird in a net by the time Sariel returned.

"You hopeless little demon." She jumped on the bed and tore the fabric right off his back, devouring his chest with heavy kisses and fierce bites.

"Yes!" he called out.

"Are you ready?" Sariel rose to her knees. She reached back to pinch the zipper on her dress. The spaghetti straps both slipped down, but she held the top up as she gave Naberius a sly, seductive smile.

"God yes," he moaned, eyes fixed on her chest.

She pulled the dress over her head, and the entire room lit up with her wonderful glow. It still hurt Naberius's eyes a little, but he didn't care. He refused to take his gaze off her. Sariel pinned his wrists up over his head, and leaning forward, they laughed in the joy of the moment before kissing. Sariel used her tongue to pry apart Naberius's lips so she could deepen the kiss. Naberius moaned—after the pain of hell and the frustration of Lust's ministrations, Sariel's weight on his hard cock was a blessing.

He hitched up, and Sariel rocked down in order to give his cock more friction. Naberius cursed God for ever giving angels androgynous bodies, but at least there was one thing he could do to make Sariel feel as good as she made him feel. He pulled away from her grip and sat them both upright. For a moment, Naberius held her waist and continued to French kiss her. Then, he moved to her neck and sucked until blasphemous, purple welts marred her dovelike skin. Naberius's fingers twitched. Eager to caress the soft down of Sariel's wings, he slid his hands up her body and toyed with the flight feathers at the tips.

She wailed in pleasure and frustration. He knew she wanted his fingers deep within her feathers, but he was drawing it out until the last moment. She started hitching in a fast, wild rhythm against his cock in an attempt to coax him to return the favor, but he only brushed the end feathers with the tips of his fingers. She started to grunt and bit her bottom lip as the tension mounted.

"Please," she begged. "Touch me."

"No." He kissed along her collarbone.

"Please, Naberius!"

"Hmm…" Naberius spider-walked his fingers up the centerline of a long, broad feather and then circled his thumbs close to the skin beneath.

"Fuck! Yes! More!" She grabbed his cock, giving her fist a little twist each time she stroked.

Naberius started panting. His fingers pulled at her feathers out of reflex, and she hissed in pleasure. Sariel jumped off the bed and grabbed Naberius's calves so she could pull him to the edge. Dropping to her knees, she plunged her mouth around Naberius's cock and sucked as hard as she could.

"Holy shit." Naberius took a sharp breath into his lungs.

As soon as her wet mouth touched his cockhead, he was lost. Any thoughts of drawing the night out disappeared as she started to bob her head. His fingers curled into soft, white feathers. He pulled them into a chaotic mess, and then smoothed them with his palms. He scratched through them to tease the skin and brought up a knee so more of his body could rub against her. She whimpered as best she could with her mouth around his cock. Her light was bright and blinding, but he could still see the way her face flushed and lips swelled as she sucked him.

"Sariel," he whispered her name in a voice gruff with emotion. "I want to come in your mouth."

Her eyes flicked up to his, and she took him deeper, all the way to the base. He raked his fingers through her wings again, paying special attention to the ridge at the top because he knew that was her favorite spot to be groomed. She shivered, and the vibrations of her moans were enough to make Naberius come with her.

"YOU SURE THIS is okay? You're not just doing this for me?"

"I-I've never done anything similar to this, but..." Jackson stared at the silk scarf in Alel's hands. "I'm kind of excited."

"If it's not fun, I'll take it off," Alel said. Jackson nodded and closed his eyes as Alel tied the scarf over his eyes. "How does that feel?"

"Fine." Jackson gave him a nervous chuckle. "I feel a little silly."

"You're sexy. Want me to take a picture before I start so you can look at it later?"

"With your cell phone." Jackson smirked. "I still don't trust you with my camera. Although, since we're married, I guess I'll have plenty of time to teach you."

"Does *teaching me* involve more personal photo shoots?"

"I do have some ideas." Jackson grinned.

"Ready for the rope?" Alel asked.

"Where should I put my hands?"

"Rest them over your head."

Jackson lay in the center of the bed and raised his arms over his head. Alel nodded and threaded the white satin rope around Jackson's wrists. Once Jackson was in a double bind, Alel tied Jackson's feet to the bedpost. He took a moment to admire Jackson. Alel's gaze trailed down the cut of Jackson's chest to his stomach, and then followed his Adonis belt to the silky black boxers he'd chosen to wear for the evening. They matched the blindfold. The white rope and black cloth were a beautiful contrast, especially against the perfect background of Jackson's brown skin.

"Are you comfortable?" he asked as he snapped a few shots with his cell phone.

"I'm good." Jackson nodded his head. "Are you sure you've never done this? Bondage is pretty kinky. I can't imagine you being shy about it even before you learned how to kiss."

"Trust me." Alel smiled. "What I'm about to do to you is going to be the sweetest, most gentle torture you've ever imagined and not something you'd find in a porn video."

"Don't leave me in suspense any longer." Jackson smiled and giggled. "Start already."

"I already have." Alel hovered his hand over Jackson's chest but didn't touch him, not yet. "I'm staring at every inch of you. You're so beautiful I can't help myself."

Jackson squirmed a little. His face beamed at Alel's statement. Alel lowered his hands, not enough to touch, but enough for Jackson to sense the warmth of them. Jackson hitched up, anticipating Alel's touch, but the touch never came, so Jackson exhaled a loud breath and settled back down. Alel meandered his way up Jackson's body until he reached Jackson's face. He almost touched Jackson's lips, making Jackson gasp and tilt his head back.

When he finally brushed his fingertips against Jackson's skin, there was only the barest hint of pressure up the curves of his cheeks. Jackson moaned. His mouth was too tempting not to taste, so Alel traced the tip of his tongue along the bottom outline of Jackson's lower lip. He finished with a soft kiss to the corner of Jackson's mouth and then used his fingers to tease Jackson's lips. Jackson relaxed his jaw, and when Alel's fingers got too close to the center of Jackson's mouth, he darted out his tongue and licked Alel's fingertips. Alel used his wet fingertips to smooth across the entire outline of Jackson's lips. Jackson snapped his lips over Alel's fingers and sucked. Alel indulged in the warmth of Jackson's mouth and then pulled his hand away. With his other hand, he cupped Jackson's face and whispered in his ear.

"I love you."

"Alel," Jackson whispered Alel's name and then moaned again when Alel drew a line down Jackson's sternum. "Okay...okay... I think I'm into the whole blindfold thing. This is turning me on."

Alel chuckled and used the tip of his nose to draw circles and letters against Jackson's chest. He gave one of Jackson's hard nipples a quick lick, but only enough to make Jackson want more, then he kissed his way to Jackson's stomach while his fingers ghosted up Jackson's ribs. Alel wandered higher and licked Jackson's other nipple three times before sucking and making Jackson call out.

He pushed himself away and examined the tray he had set out beside the bed. Alel grabbed a feather and toyed with Jackson's inner thigh. Alel saw Jackson's cock twitch through the black silk boxers, and Alel smiled. He fluttered the feather up Jackson's thigh and over his cock. He doubted Jackson noticed the light tickle through the fabric, but it was a lovely sight all the same. Alel focused on areas where he thought Jackson would be the most sensitive. He twirled the feather near Jackson's inner elbow and wrists, along his pectoral muscles, and across his lips. Jackson's chest rose and fell with excited breaths. He kept guessing where Alel would touch next, and sometimes Alel would trick him and go somewhere else, but sometimes he'd satisfy Jackson's guess and let the feather fall right where Jackson thought it would.

When Jackson grew accustomed to the feather, Alel set it aside and dragged his lips over Jackson's body. He increased the pressure of his kisses and pulled long, heated moans from Jackson's mouth. Alel straddled Jackson and eased his weight down on Jackson's silk-covered cock.

"How's this? Too much?"

"No! No." Jackson shouted the first time and then repeated in a calmer voice. "It's good. Stay there. I—oh god, Alel, please touch me."

He knew exactly what Jackson wanted, but instead of touching his cock, he kissed his mouth. It was enough for

Jackson, who whimpered into the kiss and lifted his head to make sure each kiss was rich, deep, and passionate. Alel gave his hips an experimental roll, and Jackson met the movement with his own thrust. They called back and forth to each other with their hips as their lips continued to press close. Jackson sucked at Alel's bottom lip as he pulled away so he could pant as they ground together.

Alel lifted up, grabbed a rose, and teased Jackson's sweating stomach with the petals. He concentrated on Jackson's thighs and the soles of his feet and dragged the rose up Jackson's calves. Jackson twisted at each touch as he tested his binds and gasped each time Alel hit a particularly sensitive area.

"I know you want to come," Alel hummed, still toying with Jackson's body. "But before I untie you, I want to tease you just a little longer."

"Will you take off the blindfold? I want to watch."

Alel dropped the flower to the side and reached behind Jackson's head to undo the knot keeping the blindfold in place. Jackson's face beamed when he saw Alel, and their mouths crashed together in another volley of kisses. Alel reached over and pulled a tickler from his tray of various toys.

"Not that one," Jackson said.

"No? Which one do you want me to use?" Alel asked.

"Your tail." Jackson bit his bottom lip and gave Alel a lidded stare. "You don't have the barb anymore, and the tuft at the end tickles in a nice way."

Alel's tail already swung from side to side in excitement as he worked Jackson into a frenzy. It was hard for Alel to grab and keep it still enough to use it for sensation play. Alel shuddered the moment he touched Jackson's skin. The tip wasn't sensitive, but the *thought* of using his fringe to tease

Jackson was enough to make Alel sigh in pleasure. Alel spread his wings wider so Jackson could stare at them while he teased Jackson's chest. Emboldened by the bright, yearning look in Jackson's eyes, Alel tried slipping his tail up the leg of Jackson's boxers.

"Yes!" Jackson shouted. "Hmmm...hmmmm... Alel, take them off."

"All right." Alel untied Jackson's feet and slipped the boxers off his legs. He kissed Jackson's inner thighs and sucked near the juncture of Jackson's leg and groin. Alel blew against Jackson's swollen cockhead. When Jackson's dick twitched in response, he gave it a quick lick.

"I can't take it anymore. I really can't." Jackson whined, his voice desperate. "Please Alel, please."

Alel sighed, the taste of ambrosia on his tongue from Jackson's love and eagerness, his desire and the intimacy between them. It was a new and wonderful flavor, and he knew nothing else would ever satisfy him again. He unbound Jackson's hands. Jackson reached out and ran his palms against Alel's wings until Alel called out. Then he held Alel's face and brought their mouths together. They kissed and moaned and kissed again. Alel called out when Jackson grabbed his cock.

"Grab mine," Jackson whispered.

Jackson's flesh was hot and thick in Alel's hand. They stroked together and allowed their tips to brush back and forth from the movements of their hands. Alel's tail caressed Jackson's thigh, his wings giving a broad flap in excitement. Jackson whimpered as his climax drew close. He kept his stare fixed on Alel, but at the last second, closed his eyes as he succumbed to the moment. Seeing, hearing, and sensing Jackson's orgasm brought Alel to his own, the breath stuttering in his throat as he came until he collapsed.

"That was...unlike anything I've ever imagined." Jackson panted, nuzzling against Alel's left wing.

"Mmm...you can pick what we do tomorrow." Alel bumped their noses together.

"Back rubs?" Jackson suggested.

"Sounds phenomenal." Alel pressed against the crook of Jackson's neck and kissed his throat. "Can we stay like this a moment?"

"Hmmm, yes." Jackson closed his eyes, and Alel listened to their heartbeats until they both fell asleep.

THEY DECIDED TO eat the pizza in the living room. Alel curled up in Jackson's lap, which was his favorite place in all the world to be.

"We've had it wrong this whole time. Instead of a demon, you're a housecat," Sariel commented before blowing steam away from her first slice.

"If that's an insult, you're going to have to do better." Alel curled closer to Jackson's chest. "I have no shame about how happy I am curled up with Jackson."

"Good." She smiled at him. "And you haven't had any trouble?"

"Lust seems to have given up, and I don't think most demons can even come near me," Alel confessed. "I'm too bright."

"Sometimes he's so bright I can see it through his glamour." Jackson kissed the crown of his head. "We saw an angel the other day staring. They didn't know what to make of us, and two days earlier a werewolf kept blowing his nose and then sniffing the air. I finally explained to him nothing was wrong with his nose. He looked relieved."

"I found a few other minor demons who have experimented with dating," Naberius said. "We're going to have quite the underground scene before long."

"All seven Sins will be pissed when they realize all the earthbound demons are starting to revolt."

"The archangels will also be mad once they realize how many angels are sick of standing near humans and praying instead of actually doing something to help." Sariel snorted. "A few of us are thinking about walking the streets at night and jumping in any time we see someone who needs help."

"Not without me you don't." Naberius scowled.

"She has a flaming sword, Naberius. How are *you* going to protect her?" Jackson snorted.

"At least let me try." Naberius sulked, taking a bite of his pizza. "Okay, you're right, Alel, this actually is good."

"Of course. Jackson makes the best."

"It's still not as delicious as a good blow job," Naberius insisted.

Jackson started laughing. "I know what you *meant*, but it sounded wrong."

"Maybe I meant it wrong."

"You probably did. You usually do." Jackson shook his head.

"So what are we watching?" Sariel asked.

"We usually watch horror movies," Jackson answered.

Sariel scrunched up her face. "After seeing hell?"

"True, nothing in a movie's going to be as scary as that." Jackson frowned. "I swear I'll be pissed if hell ruined me from horror for the rest of my life."

"What's this?" Alel nodded toward the television screen. "It has some good special effects. The fire coming from the dragon's mouth looks—"

"Wait, this is the news!" Jackson shouted. He grabbed Alel's waist so he could lean forward without toppling Alel off his lap.

All four of them stared a moment while the golden dragon on the screen spun in the air and then spiraled back to the ground. He changed back into a human form and then began talking into the news reporter's microphone.

"Did that dragon out himself on national television?" Jackson's mouth dropped in shock.

"Well, guess angels and demons aren't the only ones tired of the way things are." Naberius snorted. "Good thing we're all banished to Earth. I have a feeling this place is about to get really interesting."

"Does this mean we can go out without your stupid glamour on?" Jackson grinned.

Alel smiled and then turned back to the screen with a frown. "I don't know. Maybe I'll see how humans react to a dragon before I start walking around without my glamour."

"Fuck it. I'm never wearing a glamour again." Naberius took another bite of his pizza. "I never cared what humans thought, anyway."

"You might care if they throw holy water in your face," Alel said.

"A little blessed water won't hurt me. I've kissed holier things." He winked at Sariel.

"It'd still be annoying. Imagine having to walk around in wet clothing because some zealot got carried away."

"You don't have to, if you don't want to." Jackson kissed the side of Alel's head. "But I do love seeing you without the disguise."

"It would be nice." Alel stared at the television screen. The station replayed the clip of the dragon over and over. "To walk around and be myself. Isn't that what I've been trying to learn to do this whole time?"

"Well, I'm willing to try it." Sariel stood up, her hands smoothing her dress. "We were going to go bowling later, anyway, right? Let's go right now—glamours optional."

"It'll be interesting to see if they even let us play." Naberius shrugged.

Alel looked down at himself curled up in Jackson's lap. He could see his tail and pale white arms spotted with lavender freckles, and although he couldn't see them, he knew the pointed ears, horns, and wings were there—it was all a part of him. Alel never experienced sunlight directly on his skin without the familiar restriction of a glamour covering his body.

Except once.

The day Jackson said I love you the first time. Alel had removed his glamour so he could kiss Jackson without hiding behind any magic.

"All right." Alel crawled off Jackson's lap. "Might as well see what happens."

Jackson squealed and jumped to his feet. He lifted Alel into his arms and spun him around. Alel laughed, dizzy by the third spin, or perhaps it was the following kisses tilting his thoughts off-balance. Hand in hand, they stepped out the door and onto the street. Alel's tail curled and uncurled as they walked along the sidewalk. He stretched out his wings and enjoyed the sun's rays against them. Alel drew a deep breath into his chest, holding it before releasing the air from his lungs. The chance to live as his true self, to never again shroud himself in pretty lies, excited him. Jackson squeezed their clasped hands, and Alel smiled.

About the Author

Hey there, readers. It's me, ya boi, Sita Bethel. And this is a biography where I tell you all the boring facts about my life—how I have a degree in writing, and how my two cats, Odin and Anpu, will one day rule this land as your feline overlords. Enough of that same old, same old. Here's the real dirt. Sita Bethel wraps up like a burrito with a weighted blanket. They host coloring parties as a personal eff-you to anxiety, and read everything from trash British sensationalist novels like *The Moonstone* by Wilkie Collins to literary masterpieces such as *The Color Purple* by Alice Walker. Had enough of Sita Bethel yet? If not, check out @sita_bethel on Twitter, or sitabethelfiction on Facebook, or even www.sitabethel.com.

Email: stiabethel@gmail.com

Facebook: www.facebook.com/sitabethelfiction

Twitter: @sita_bethel

Website: www.sitabethel.com

Other books by this author

"Angels in Delaware" within Beneath the Layers
Anthology
"Dressed in Wolf Skin" within Into the Mystic, Volume
Two
"Master Thief" within Once Upon a Rainbow, Volume Two
Cold Like Snow

Also Available from NineStar Press

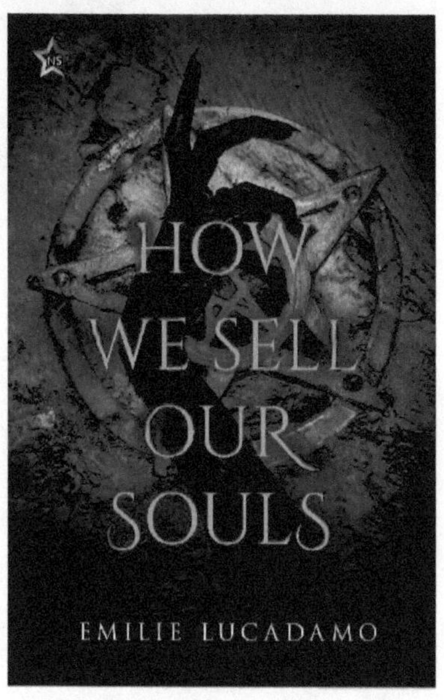

Connect with NineStar Press

Website: NineStarPress.com

Facebook: NineStarPress

Facebook Reader Group: NineStarNiche

Twitter: @ninestarpress

Tumblr: NineStarPress